CHURCHBOYS AND OTHER SINNERS

CHURCHBOYS

&

OTHER SINNERS

By Preston L. Allen

CAROLINA WREN PRESS • DURHAM, NORTH CAROLINA

Several of these stories have appeared in earlier form in the following magazines:
Seattle Review, "The Lord of Travel"; *Crab Orchard Review*, "Is Randy Roberts There?";
Drumvoices, "Get Some."

Library of Congress Cataloging-in-Publication Data
Allen, Preston L., 1964-
 Churchboys and other sinners / by Preston L. Allen.– 1st ed.
     p. cm.
"Sonja H. Stone Prize in Fiction."
 ISBN 0-932112-44-7 (alk. paper)
1. United States–Social life and customs–Fiction. 2. African
Americans–Fiction. I. Title.
 PS3601.L435C47 2003
 813'.6–dc21

*This publication was made possible in part by generous grants from the North Carolina Arts
Council. In addition, we gratefully acknowledge the ongoing support made possible through gifts
to the Durham Arts Council's United Arts Fund as well as grants from the City of Durham.*

Book Design and Photography: Martha Scotford
Cover Art and Design: Stephanie Werts
Author Photo: Roland Joynes

Carolina Wren Press, 120 Morris Street, Durham, NC 27701
www.carolinawrenpress.org

ACKNOWLEDGEMENTS:

To David Kellogg, Andrea Selch, and the generous people at Carolina Wren Press: Much gratitude.

To Ellen Milmed, my editor: Thank you!!

To my teachers: Lynne Barrett, who taught me to hear my own voice, taught it to sing; Les Standiford, who taught me what a story is, and how to tell one; James W. Hall, who taught me what an audience is, and how to keep one; John Dufresne, who taught me to shake the page until all the weak words fell off, then shake it again; Campbell McGrath, who taught me to see sounds, taste whispers, hear shapes, smell colors; Meri-Jane Rochelsen, who taught me to read and read and read; and Jean J. Eargle, who read and read and read everything I wrote.

To the gang at the F.I.U. Friday Night workshop, especially Sally, Jesse, Laura, Ellen, Tony, Richard, Howard, and the other Howard.

To my loyal readers and supporters, Cameron Allen, William E. Durnell, Josett Peat, Tony Simonette, Stewart Allen, Humberto V. Allen, and Edgar Allen— I hope I can be there for you as you were there for me.

To Jason Murray, Geoffrey Philp, Kevin Eady, Lee Kline, Louise Skellings, Elena Perez-Mirabal, Ivonne Lamazares, Ariel Gonzalez, and Sherwin Allen, who saw these things when they were raw and did not run away.

To my father, for giving me storytelling gifts.

To my mother, for being my gift.

TABLE OF CONTENTS

Is Randy Roberts There?

*M*en are little piglets, don't you know? They just are.

Four months ago, I find myself at the Cove. It's reggae night, and the crowd is a mixture of buppies and beeper bandits—the black young urban professional and the conspicuously criminal. I am sitting at a table with one of the latter when I make eye contact with one of the former. A pretty boy, kicking it out there on the dance floor.

My eyes follow his graceful form like search lights in the semi-dark. He's big and beautiful. Is he dancing alone? That ain't right. I'd like to say, "Come here, I'll dance with you, maybe more," but instead I say the obligatory "No kidding?" to the little beeper bandit who's been dogging me all night.

"No kidding?" I say, testing the liqueur the short man has bought me in his hopeless attempt to pick me up. It is bitter like pine leaves.

He says, "I drives a Mercedes," and passes me his key ring (yep, a Mercedes). He folds his arms confidently, nods his head in time to the rhythm, squints seductively through contact lenses that turn his eyes an arresting green. "This brother get paid in full," he says.

And I go, "No kidding?" I'm trapped. Looking at "this brother who get paid in full" is painful, and he's managed to keep me looking at him most of the night. Ugly? Try FUGLY. The only thing good about his face is that his green-light-go! eyes are white where they are supposed to be white. I'm thinking, Christmas tree. I'm thinking, Greensleeves. I'm thinking, The green grass grows all around and around and the green grass grows all around. I take another swig of the horrible liqueur, shiver, and fight not to spit it back into the glass.

"No kidding?"

"In full, baby."

"No kidding?" I say, turning to smile at the pretty boy, who smiles back from across the frenetic oblivion of the room. He's taller than everyone around him. That's good. I like tall. I am tall. I hope he doesn't think the little evergreen here is my lover.

"And I'm materialistic," he says, bringing a fist to his pursed lips, kissing his large rings, one on every finger, two on the thumb. Imagine that. "And I treats my ladies right." Now his pink tongue flicks out from behind two rows of gold teeth, and licks a thumb ring suggestively. "I treats them RIGHT."

"Materialistic? No kidding?"

He reaches for me. I avoid his beringed clutch by thrusting the terrible drink into his hand. I say, "This is a little too strong for me. I wonder if you can get me something else."

My cavalier takes the drink and says, "I'll get you something a little bit more gentler," and the way he hangs on the word "gentler" I can tell he thinks something a little bit more specialer has passed between us.

With a suggestive wink, he pops up from his chair and pushes to the bar through the dark bodies that twist and writhe on the dance floor, and I think about making my escape, but I don't because I still have his car keys. I'm sure that's why he left them with me. He is of a predictable type of piglet.

Oink.

Night clubs are their mud holes. Bars are their slop troughs. Women are their pearls. Useless. Less desirable than apple core or corn husk. Something to wear around their fat necks as they grovel in the dung. I know all this and still I make the club scene.

Aunt Celia, who raised me, says the only place I'll ever find a good one is at school, at work, or at church, which leaves me no prospects because I've long since graduated, I work as a counselor at a women's crisis center (think about it), and I don't do the church thing anymore—not after Pastor Paul dumped me for his wife.

And I'm 32.

So, yeah, I do the clubs. I got used to the squealing.

I give the pretty boy plenty of opportunity to make his move by sending the persistent short man on every errand I can think of:

A strawberry daiquiri—

"You sure can drink for a pretty gal."

A pack of LifeSavers—

"I likes a woman with a sweet mouth."

A song by Shaba—

"The DJ is my cut buddy," he boasts. "He'll play anything I tell him."

But the pretty boy ignores me all night. Then when the club is about to close and the short man is away on an errand of his own—"somebody important just beeped me"—the pretty boy pushes up, his handsome, thick-lipped face posing rudely in the dim lights.

He wears a Morehouse College ring on the wedding finger. His suit looks expensive, but his shoes, though well polished, are the bland type a man is more likely to wear to work than to a club. Is he practical or poor? He is tall, but is he taller than my six-feet-one in flats?

It doesn't matter because Prettyboy doesn't offer me a drink or a ride home. He just hands me this phone number written on the back of a gum wrapper.

"I'm Johnny," he says. "Call me." And then he leaves.

Now you know that ain't right. What does he take me for?

Oink. Squeal.

The short man makes his way back to the table holding one jeweled hand over his mouth, his apologetic eyes betraying that he has terrible news for me.

"I'm busted," he confesses. Laughing hopelessly, he points to his beeper. "That was my baby momma Doretha what called me."

He thinks my perturbed expression is meant for him, so he continues.

"This other gal I used to be with name Nancy, she been calling Doretha telling her that I'm her baby daddy too, and Doretha say she gonna kick Nancy ass and mine too if it's true, and as much as I would like to take you to a nice motel tonight and rub you down . . . MMMM . . . you look so good."

"That's quite all right," I say, squeezing Johnny's gum wrapper in my fist.

"MMMM . . . I'll give you my beeper number."

"That's quite all right."

"MMMM . . . baby, don't be mad with me." The short man takes out a business card—a business card!—places it on the table when I won't take it from him. "Call me and I'll make it up to you . . . in a BIG way . . . MMMM."

The short man kisses me on the forehead and then leaves.

I'm thinking, I hopes Doretha and Nancy be kicking your ass tonight.

I spend the next day in a funk.

Should I call the nervy son-of-a-bitch?

I'm not calling him, I say. Let him rot.

Who does he think he is, this "Johnny?" Should I call him?

So what if I call him? What then? No, I'm not calling him.

I'm educated, I'm attractive, I'm sensual, I'm sensuous, and at 32 I'm inexplicably single.

I'm a pearl.

He's a porker.

Should I call him?

All day I'm like this. The wrapper doesn't leave my hand. Suddenly, around 10 p.m., I call him. I hate him, but I call him. I decide I'm calling him only to put him in his place.

"Hello," I say. "Is Johnny there?"

An old woman's cracking voice: "Yes."

His mother, I guess. He lives with his mother, what does this mean? I notice no one is speaking.

"Hello," I repeat. "Is Johnny there?"

"Yes," the voice cracks again. Then there is silence once more.

OK. OK. I see what's happening. The waiting game.

She knows damned well I want to speak with Johnny, so I refuse to say, "Well, can I speak with him?" But the silence continues—I mean for like a minute—until I finally say:

"Well, can I speak with him?"

"It's very late," she says.

Ten o'clock? I say nothing because really I can't believe this is happening. A grown man.

But she says nothing either, and silence melts into profounder silence.

It is the same waiting game I played with Sister Paul during the two months she and Pastor Paul were officially separated but still living together so as not to upset the congregation. I played the waiting game with Sister Paul because I knew she was trying to intimidate me. A turf thing. If I ever hoped to win her man, I had to show her I was patient, strong.

I play the waiting game now with Johnny's mother because I am so stunned by her audacity that I can't move the phone from my ear, can't close my gaping jaw. But I can play a mean waiting game. I wait and I wait. I'm not going away. She'd better understand. Finally, she says, "I'll get him. But this is the last time."

I win again.

Before he picks up the line, I hear an exchange of shouts.

". . . women calling this late at night!"

"Momma, please!"

". . . thought I raised you better than that!"

"Momma!"

I'm hooked. I've got to find out what this Johnny person is all about.

"Johnny here."

"Hi, Johnny. This is Monique. We met at the Cove last . . ."

"I know where we met. What do you want? It's real late."

Stunned, I say, "You gave me your . . . Didn't you say to call?"

"Just give me your number, and I'll call you back tomorrow."

I give him my number knowing it isn't supposed to work like this.

Aunt Celia says the fine, good-looking ones are aloof. You're the one who has to approach them, beg for their company, and all you end up with is a few nights of passionless intimacy and a polite goodbye when they leave you for someone else—an ex-wife, ex-girlfriend, some new woman who is just like (God forbid) their dear old momma. Then again, the mashed-up ones offer you the world—their dysfunctional version of it at any rate—poverty, abuse, drugs, scandal. And when you don't take it, they act like you're the one crazy. School, work, and church, she insists, are the only safe places.

But I blew my chances in college. I was virtuous, thank you. Actually, I was an empty shell. The great love of my life had already sucked everything out of me, and I'm not talking about Pastor Paul. He came later.

And work? I don't eat where I shit.

And church? I'm not taking that Thou Shalt Not crap from any vainglorious, megalomaniac preacher man ever again, no matter how much I love him. Now I'm talking about Pastor Paul. The lech.

So I do the clubs.

When Johnny Geckle—how's that for a name?—calls the next day, our conversation is friendly but brief.

"I'm sorry about Momma," he says. "She's eighty. She's a little screwy at times."

The seed does not fall far from the tree. Shut up, Aunt Celia.

"Eighty?" I say. "How old are you?"

"Your age. Momma had me late in life."

"And your father?"

"You're very pretty, Monique," he says, which is flattering but not an answer to the question—a question that's innocent enough but I probably have no business asking. If his mother is eighty, his father might have died many years before. Or is his father alive? A young stud who knocked up and then abandoned his ancient bride? Perhaps for Johnny this is a tough subject to talk about.

"I can't wait to see you again," he adds.

And I agree to go out with him just like that.

He is confident in a way I've never encountered before, and yet there is something about him that speaks of innocence. Also, it doesn't take a genius to figure out Johnny Geckle is hiding something. But what?

Questions. Questions.

This, I realize, is his appeal.

So four days later I'm inspecting myself in the hallway mirror as I wait for Johnny Geckle to pick me up for our first date.

I'm wearing this red blouse that's more like a bikini top made of spandex than a blouse. I can't decide how it looks, especially with the two pounds I've gained due to my tendency to overeat when I'm nervous—and Johnny Geckle has made me very nervous. I decide to cover the blouse by wearing it under a short jacket. Just enough of my smooth stomach and my perfect "inny" belly-button shows. My hair hangs in a long ponytail to the small of my back. I look ravishing, but the thing I suspect is hottest about me is my new skirt, which cost $200 and fits like a second layer of soft, black, leathery skin.

I admire my profile. Standing tall in my spiked heels, I am slender, I am statuesque. Or am I gawky? Am I an ostrich? They called me ostrich in high school. I had no boyfriends in high school. Not one single one. Even fat girls had boyfriends. But not me, the ostrich with her head buried in the books.

But I had feelings. And eyes. And I could see Randy Roberts, his pretty eyes, his lanky frame, the basketball player, a boy who could look down on me as tall as I was. The love of my life, Randy never said a word to me. He sat ahead of me in chemistry and that became my favorite class. All those nights I went to sleep dreaming about him, then I get this note: "I've always loved you. Tomorrow in class, I want to show you how much I love you. I want to kiss you in front of everyone. Please wear something nice. Make me proud. Love Randy."

Wear something nice? Upon my insistence, Aunt Celia maxed out a credit card on a new dress, new shoes—with heels, I could wear heels with Randy!—perfume, lipstick, and Aunt Celia stayed up half the night getting the Curly Perm to set right in my hair.

The next day . . . the next day, Randy Roberts' seat was empty. He had transferred to another school. Yesterday had been his last day. His friends who were in on the joke sure got a kick out of it—me, all dressed up, too dressed up, really, for the chemistry test I failed.

Randy Roberts was the first little piglet. Does he have any idea how he screwed up my life? Does he have any idea that he made me a criminal? For the next four years I was a crank caller. For hours at a time, I'd pick up the phone, dial a number, and say, "Hello, is Randy Roberts there?"

"No, wrong number."

"Thank you. I'm sorry." Click. Dial, dial, dial. "Hello, is Randy Roberts there?"

And sometimes a Randy Roberts would answer—this happened 127 times—but never the right Randy Roberts. Nevertheless, I would curse him out until he hung up. He deserved it, having a name like that.

Thank God, I'm better now. Thanks to Pastor Paul. Yep.

At any rate, I don't want to be an ostrich with Johnny Geckle, so I change to flats. And I wait.

He is late.

Little pig, little pig, where the hell are you?

When he arrives an hour later, I'm wearing my spiked heels again.

I open the door. He stands there in the polished work shoes that he wore to the Cove, a pair of faded jeans, and a white shirt buttoned at the neck. He looks me over. He puts his hand to his mouth and chuckles.

Squirming, I consider staying home.

Behind Johnny, I see a late model pickup. It is red with whitewall tires and tinted windows. The flatbed is filled with garbage cans and garbage bags stuffed with leaves and branches.

My god. Johnny Geckle is a lawn man.

I'm not dressed for yard work.

By way of explanation which explains nothing, he says, "I had to pick up Momma from the clinic," and he turns around and heads for the truck. I follow him, my heels clicking on the cement walkway.

I notice I'm about an inch taller than Johnny Geckle. I really ought to stay home.

He helps me into the cab of the truck, his grip firm, strong, his palms soft. He reminds me to buckle up, and then he slams my door. I buckle up.

When he starts the engine, the bluesy strains of B. B. King's "Nobody Home" flow from the speaker on his side of the cab while loud static buzzes from the speaker on my side. "It's broken," he explains, but does not turn down the radio or transfer the output to the one speaker that is working.

Thanks for considering me, Johnny Geckle.

We drive.

He's all torso. I'm all leg. The truck doesn't fit. My knees are pressed up against the glove compartment. I move the seat back as far as it will go, and that helps a little. I remove my shoes. That doesn't help at all. I notice my stockings are beginning to strand, and I put my shoes back on. I twist in my seat trying to find a comfortable position. The gearshift prevents me from shifting far enough to my left, and my skirt is so short that if I shift far enough to the right to be comfortable I will give Johnny Geckle an indecent view. So I sit with my knees pressed against the glove compartment and steel myself for a date so utterly bad it will give Aunt Celia a year's worth of things to warn me about.

Watch out for quiet men. Watch out for men over thirty who live with their mothers. Watch out for men who drive trucks. Watch out for men who own one pair of shoes.

Then, we start talking, and I'm not so certain.

Yes, he is a lawn man, but—

"I make my own hours."

And yes, he lives at home with his mother, but—

"Momma. What can I say? She worries about me. I protect the women in my life."

—and he did graduate from college.

"I'm working on my Ph.D. in mathematics. I want to be an actuary."

"Will you work in banking, insurance, or private consulting?" I ask.

"Insurance." He turns to me. "I'm surprised you know what an actuary is. And pleased. Most people have never heard of us, although without us . . ."

". . . 'Business as we know it in America would come to an abrupt and permanent halt.'" I quote the article I recently read in *Newsweek* where I first encountered the word "actuary." I add, "Actuaries make a lot of money."

"They sure do," he says, winking at me, his lucky girl.

But I wonder. . . if Johnny is going for his Ph. D., he must have his master's already. According to the article, an actuary with a bachelor's degree can make over $30,000 a year. Certainly, one with a master's can make a good deal more. Why is Johnny Geckle a yard man?

At a light, he reaches for my hand.

"I'm beginning to see I was right about you, Monique." His hand is soft. I can't imagine anyone with such a soft hand making a living cutting hedges. He says, "I wanted to approach you from the moment I spotted you at the Cove. But there was that guy."

"The little guy? A total stranger," I say.

The light changes, and Johnny withdraws his hand so that he can resume driving with both hands on the steering wheel, left hand at twelve o'clock, right hand at three. "But I'm kind of shy. And you were so beautiful, so statuesque [his word, I swear it!] that I thought you would insult some average-looking guy like me trying to talk to you. Even now I feel overshadowed by your enchanting [yes, his word!] beauty."

I look at Johnny, who's not average-looking at all. And he's beginning to make me feel pretty good too, even if he does drive five miles under the speed limit. I begin to forget the garbage bags full of branches and leaves riding behind us in the flat bed.

"I've learned to be direct and abrupt. Rejection doesn't hurt as much if it's over with quickly."

"I know what you mean."

"No you don't. I refuse to believe a stunning woman like you has ever been rejected."

God bless me. I like this Johnny. I forget about my aching knees and concentrate on his dark eyebrows, strong jaw, sensuous profile. Not at all average-looking. Johnny Geckle is not average in any way. I bet his mother is responsible for his feelings of inferiority.

What a monster she must be.

At another light, Johnny says, "My mother is a monster."

"No kidding," I say. I'm getting the hang of Johnny Geckle.

We stop at our destination, a movie theater. It is not where I hoped he would take me on our first date, I really don't want to go inside dressed as I am, but Johnny is nice and cute and perhaps poor, and he has a future and he thinks I'm statuesque, and we're getting along so well I'm beginning to think—dare I dream it?—he is the one.

Just as I'm about to forget that Johnny is a man and men are fond of mud, he pays for his ticket with a handful of change and a crumpled dollar bill he digs out of his front pocket, and then he walks into the lobby—without me.

He doesn't even look back.

Through the glass door I see him buying something at the concession stand.

I pay for my ticket with the emergency cash Aunt Celia encourages me to carry. Don't depend on them for anything, she says. Be able to pay your own way.

Behind me, I hear someone say, "I thought they were together."

Oink.

When my statuesque butt storms into the lobby, it is ready to slap one Johnny Geckle repeatedly in the face. So what he is poor and has one pair of shoes? So what his father is dead? So what he lives with a hag?

But Johnny Geckle hands me a Coke and keeps the hotdog for himself, and he leads me into the semi-dark auditorium where I am reluctant to make a scene. "There's a really great plot twist in this movie," he says, wiping mustard from his mouth with the back of his hand. "The hairdresser is a transsexual." He licks the mustard from his hand.

What is your plot twist, Johnny Geckle? Will I strangle you tonight, or will I invite you in for a drink? Will I invite you in for a drink and then strangle you?

Johnny Geckle quite disarms me.

I soon find my anger gone, although Aunt Celia's voice is screaming in my head, Don't go easy on him because he's a simpleton! You let him get away with it once, he'll do it again and again! Beware of men who are soft in the head!

As I drink the Coke and watch the twisted film, I find the touch of Johnny Geckle's hand in the dark to be tender, and I want to cry.

I am vulnerable again.

I've never met a tender man before, tender, yet strong. Pastor Paul was all fire and brimstone, justice and righteousness, except when he removed his collar, the mystery of the Beast rising in us both. Pastor Paul was weak in the flesh. (Actually, his dick was sturdy as a piston.) What I mean was he was weak for the flesh of his flock—all of his flock—not just me in the pinkness of my youth who loved him more than I loved his version of God. "God is a God of moderation," he moaned, filling me in both word and deed. He forbid me to wear heels, except in bed. The liar. Oink. The hypocrite. Oink. The seducer of mind as well as body. Oink. The son-of-a-bitch didn't even help pay for the abortion.

Aunt Celia's warning did not save me then, and it does not save me now as I contemplate Johnny Geckle.

I am vulnerable again.

How do they do it?

I kiss him.

Johnny Geckle is not bright enough to be surprised by the kiss, just startled.

"Oh, baby," he says. Then he initiates a kiss, a better one, and just as it is getting as good as a kiss can get—the man has adventurous hands—he asks me to be still a moment, because interesting part of the film is about to occur.

Startled I am, but not surprised. I sit motionless. Thinking.

On screen, a tank runs over a black Englishman, killing him. It is a wonderful moment. Then Johnny kisses me again, his hands running over my black body like the relentless tracks of the tank. He liberates a nipple. It disappears into his mouth. I can't say that this feels good. There are people watching us. I know they are. What can I do? "You're just right for me," he says. "You're just right." Nibble. Nibble.

Am I angry? Am I excited?

I am resolved, because now I know.

He's correct. I am just right for him. I see us working yards together, him ahead in his polished shoes slashing unwanted growth with a machete; me behind him collecting it where it has fallen, bagging it, bringing in the sheaves so to speak; his harpy of a mother watching us from the back of the truck, sipping lemonade and accusing me of preventing her bright boy from getting his doctorate by giving him my breasts to suck at night when he should be resting his mind for the actuarial exams.

I am drawn to him, and the reason is simple. Johnny does not give one shit about me. I'm drawn to men who don't like me. Perhaps I don't like me too. But I should like me—I'm statuesque. Something is definitely wrong with my head.

This time it's going to be different.

I tuck myself back into my blouse. I tell Johnny I need to go to the bathroom.

"Hurry back," he says. "You don't want to miss the scene with the transsexual."

I slip out of the theater and cross the street to the mall. I hail a cab home.

I undress.

How is it that I'm wearing the thong bikini Pastor Paul gave me the Christmas before Sister Paul won him back? What was I expecting of Johnny Geckle?

Instead of crying, I take off the thong, compress it into a ball, and place it in the kitchen waste basket atop a crust of pizza and half an egg shell.

My phone does not stop ringing that night, nor for the next week, but I do not answer it. Then I exchange my phone number for an unlisted one.

I am careful to avoid leaving my home through the front door after I get up one morning and find Johnny out there asleep in his truck. Startled but not surprised, I become wary of red trucks.

I receive several letters from Johnny Geckle, and I throw them away without reading them.

All the while, I resist the urge to dial random numbers on the phone. Get over it, I tell myself. Grow up. I call Pastor Paul instead. He recognizes my voice.

"Monique, darling, I'm so glad you called," he says. "My life has been nothing without you."

"Is Randy Roberts there?"

"Monique?"

"Is Randy Roberts there?"

"Are you OK, baby?"

I emphasize each word. "IS RANDY ROBERTS THERE?"

He says, "No, Monique. It's me."

I say, "Sorry. I must have the wrong number," and hang up. I do this maybe two, three more times—not because I'm regressing, but because I find it wonderful-ly curative.

OK. Maybe five more times. Six tops.

A month later, I scarcely remember what Johnny Geckle looks like.

Four months later, I'm at the Cove, and there is Johnny Geckle in the same suit, same shoes. He sees me. I turn back to my sweet drink and the short, talkative buppie—a lawyer this time—who has bought it for me. Johnny touches me on the shoulder. Would I like to dance?

"Sure, Johnny." I tell the little attorney that I'll be right back.

The song is slow and romantic, and Johnny is a wonderful dancer.

"I'm sorry for the way I treated you."

"No, Johnny, you were just perfect." I feel his arms go around me, so tenderly. I'm aware that our groins mesh perfectly. "It was I who needed to work some things out," I say.

"I wonder if we can get together afterwards, maybe pick up where we left off at the movies?" He begins whispering in my ear. He does not speak loudly enough for me to hear anything but the texture of his words, but I know he is saying, "Can I take you home? Can I take you home? Can I . . ."

But we've already established that he's shorter than me in heels.

"How is Momma doing?" I say.

"What?" Johnny Geckle stiffens.

And I reach for his mouth with my mouth.

Too startled to be surprised, he offers his sweet lips. I taste his tongue as it slips between my lips. Our song is playing. This will be our song. I bite Johnny's tongue. He jerks away. I stumble in my heels—break a heel, but I do not fall. I look at him. He does not look back.

I return with my shoes in my hand to the short man who is guarding my drink, a below average-looking man for whom I feel nothing, and about whom I have no questions. If he gives me his beeper number, who knows, I may agree to marry him.

Get Some

"You look tired."

I ain't tired.

"You angry?"

Not angry.

"Then what's that look on your face?" she says.

Just my face. That's how my face looks.

"See how you sound? Sounds like you're angry. Or sleepy."

I ain't angry. Or sleepy.

"Then what are you with that face?"

I'm just me, I say.

She laughs, and I want to say, what I am is surly, which is what my dad calls it. But that's not even the point because right now what I am is ready to slide off my baggy jeans and get some, but you look like you wanna talk about my face or my voice or watch me move heavy furniture first or anything but let me slide off my baggy jeans and get some in the half hour left before I have to get back to third period, which is where I'm supposed to be at. So I sit on your couch and wait. All surly.

She says, "If you're tired, you don't have to do this."

I'm not tired.

"I don't want to get you in trouble."

Ain't no trouble. I'm here, right?

"You could get detention."

I'm supposed to be in detention now for what we did last week, but I'm here, right?

Her place smells like the joint she's been smoking. She don't offer. I don't ask. When she stands, finally, her dress is all rumpled. It's a faded green house dress like my mom wears when she vacuums or does laundry, but my mom does not smoke—joints or anything—though to calm her nerves she drinks a wine cooler now and then, and she would certainly need a wine cooler if she was here to see this grown woman with two children peel back her house dress and flop her titties into my eighth-grade hands, which is what she does.

I like the feel of her titties in my hands, for real. The way I work them, she closes her eyes. There's a double scar between them, twin check marks the crazy ex-boyfriend carved deep into her autumn-leaf skin with linoleum shears to teach her who is who and what is what. The good ex-boyfriend, for whose charms she had forgotten who is who and what is what, just about lost his mind when he saw the wound, and he and his li'l bro, who is his cut buddy but not really his brother or related to him by blood or nothing, hunted down and kicked the shit out of the crazy ex-boyfriend. Then made sure the crazy one got sent to jail by making her testify and holding her hand in court when she broke down and started bawling. You have to admire the good ex-boyfriend for that. And actually the good ex-boyfriend is not really ex. Yet. But he's at work, and I'm here with his girl's titties in my mouth.

She reaches for my zipper, and I lean back a little and take a breath. I'm going to get some for sure, I'm thinking. Maybe I can get some twice.

She smiles up at me from between my legs. Now that she's kissed everything down there, she's offering to do more. "Do you want me to?" she says.

Yes, I say.

And I think, it ain't my mouth.

"Here goes."

Yes!

I bury my head in her snap-on dreadlocks. I'm going to be late for third period for real.

☘ ☘ ☘

"Who you looking at like that? I asked you a question. You better answer me."

I answered already.

"Don't back talk me."

I didn't back talk you. I told you already I was trying to get my book back from this boy—

"What boy?" he roars, and mashes his face into my space, and he's a big man, which is scary but doesn't really scare me because I know principals ain't allowed to hit. "What's his name?"

This boy I go to first period with—

"What's his name? You deaf?"

I think his name—

"You think his name? You don't know him and you gave him your books? You think I was born under a tree?" He mashes his face into my space, actually touching my cheeks with his nose and mustache, which tickles, but not in a good way. "I don't like people lying to me. Especially stupid lies. You think I already forgot what security told me?"

That's what I was trying to tell Curity—I mean Mr. Roden, I say. I had played basketball with this boy in first period, but then when the bell had rang we had left, and then when I realized my book was gone, I was trying to go to his class to wait for him so I could get my book back, but then Curity—I mean Mr. Roden blew his whistle and I didn't have a hall pass and here I am.

"Is that right?"

Yes, sir.

"Who you looking at like that?"

I turn away from him and look at the walls all covered over with stupid stick drawings in different colored crayons—green, black, yellow, red, brown, white—which are supposed to be children from all nations holding hands and smiling at the wonderful free education they're getting, which is not even the point because there's only black and brown crayons at this school. I think I saw a yellow crayon at the beginning of the year, but he musta transferred. Some of the teachers are white crayons. Actually, most of the teachers are white crayons. But my principal is a big black crayon, and out the corner of my eye I see the walkie-talkie pressed against his mouth, and he's talking loud so I can hear my story contradicted by Mr. Roden, or school security, or Curity, or the good ex-boyfriend, which in fact is who he is.

No offense, Curity, but I'm getting hard right now thinking about your black crayon girlfriend who cleans the school bathrooms part-time and spends the rest of her time at home waiting, but not alone, for you, the good ex-boyfriend who's not really ex. Yet. It's not my fault. I didn't ask. She did. What was I supposed to do? I had never seen titties before. I ain't got nothing against you, brother, really. It's just that I'm surly, and people pay more attention to my face than my words, and nobody trusts me, and they should trust me because everybody needs to be trusted and it ain't my fault that sometimes I have to lie. What am I supposed to do? Tell everybody I smoke joints? Tell everybody I'm getting some from the cleaning lady? And here's this stupid wall in my face again. If I had a box of crayons, I would draw titties on all these stick-figure girls in their triangle dresses, so it's easier to tell them apart from the boys. On the boys, I would draw baggy pants.

"He told me 'bout some book or something," the principal says.

The walkie-talkie scratches back loud: "Where I found him over by the back entrance there ain't even no classrooms."

"So where was he going to get this supposed book?"

"There ain't even no classrooms over there I told you."

The principal nods his head and gives me a look. Now he's convinced, but so what? What's the most they can do to me? I'm already on detention. Another detention?

"Boy," the principal says to me, "I think you're due for a suspension."

Suspension?

"Yes." Now he's smiling all threatening-like. "Five days."

Suspension, I say, but I'm thinking, you call me stupid? What is more stupid than suspending me for not being in school? It's illogical: I cut a few classes to get some, and you punish me by allowing me to cut all of my classes. For five days! Do you have any idea how much I can get in five days with no school to get in the way? I'm going to get some and get some until my eyes cross.

I could shout Joy! and Rapture! but I don't. I look back at him all surly, which is my face in its natural state.

"And one more thing," he says, slapping the walkie-talkie against his palm. "Your father is on his way over."

I fix my face tight so that my fear does not show through my surly, which is not even the point because more than anything, I'm confused. My dad?

Totally confused.

※   ※   ※

So he's sitting next to me with my baggy-pants ass in his power tie and his pressed blue shirt and black pants and shined shoes, and he's smelling all like that cologne he wears, which makes me about to sneeze, and he's listening to the principal say again and again what I had did and how a suspension is the only way to teach me a lesson, and once in a while he looks up at the swaggering Curity in his brown uniform and his fake-ass badge and his funky specs when he says some little snippy remark to emphasize what the principal just said, and I'm thinking why did mom call him? What game is she trying to pull?

He says, "I want to hear his side of it."

"What side of it?" says Curity.

"He's been lying all day," says the principal. "Why would he change now?"

"I want to hear his side of it. He won't lie to me. We have a special relationship." And for the first time since he's arrived, my dad turns to me with this friendly expression on his face. "Tell me your side, Junior."

And I'm thinking, who are you? You try to be cool and all, but you walked out on me when I was six. I see the principal more than you. I see Curity more than you. If things work out, I'll be seeing Curity's woman more than you. Special relationship? I see you every other weekend! It's easy to mask my surly for two-and-a-half days every other week, dad.

So I look into my dad's eyes and say, I had played basketball with this boy in first period, but then when the bell had rang, we had left, and then when I realized my book was gone, I was trying to go to his class to wait for him—

"What boy?" interrupts the principal.

"There ain't no classrooms where I found you," says Curity.

"Let him talk," says my dad, and he's wearing a tie and the principal is not and Curity looks like a clown in his flashy specs, and though my father is a small man, he's already let them know that he's a teacher at a real school, a professor actually, at a college with white and yellow crayon students and only a few brown ones. He's let them know he carries more weight than they do in this teacher game they're playing. "A suspension is a serious punishment with long-term implications. I want to hear his side. Junior?"

Yes, sir?

"Were you skipping school, son?"

No, sir.

"Then what happened?"

I was trying to get this book back from this kid—

Curity snorts. The principal points his finger. "If he were my son, I would discipline him. Some people got strange methods of raising children. The old-fashioned way was better."

"I'm rearing my son my way!" And they shut up. My dad takes my hand. "Son, what is the name of the other kid?"

What kid?

"The one who had your book."

I don't know his name. I only know him from P.E.

"If you don't really know him, son, or his name, then how did you expect to find his class?"

What class?

"The one he has after P.E. You were going there, remember, to get back your book."

I'm thinking, Oh no. Which lie was I telling? But I'm cool. I recover quick.

Dad, I didn't say I knew where his class was. I said I was looking for his class. I was looking through all the classrooms to—

My dad says, "That's illogical." Then after a while: "Stupid."

Not everybody got the same logic, dad.

"What?" says my dad, squeezing my hand until it hurts. "And what's that look on your face?" He releases my hand and then stabs a finger against my forehead until it hurts real bad and I have to shrink away. "Don't you ever look at me with that look on your face."

I wipe the look away real quick, but I know I'm lost. I've never seen my dad like this. Smoke coming all out of his ears.

The principal says, "Old-fashioned discipline is always best."

And Curity, the stupid bastard, just stands there smiling like he's got something on me.

✠　✠　✠

In the car, I find myself clutching at the puffed-out pleats of my pants, which is weird because I can see my hands open and close open and close like I'm really

nervous and losing control of the situation and I can't stop them, and I can hear my
dad's lecture about how I have let him down, how he had thought so highly of me
but now he's not sure why since I'm obviously a liar which is worse than a delin-
quent, because as a kid my age I'm entitled to my share of rebellion, which after all
is what life is all about, and he should know because he was a kid once too and he
rebelled his share, but he's truly disappointed because I blew this special relationship
with him by lying to his face, forchrissake, when he was the only one in that principal's office who had my interests in mind, and it's fine to rebel once in a while, but a
boy should never lie to his father, hell, lie to your mother, lie to women in general,
but never lie to your father, so now it looks like he's going to have to do something
he never dreamed he'd have to do, and my hands are just clutching like mad at my
pants and all I can do is watch them and wonder where the control went.

"You understand me?" he says. "Boy?"

But what was I supposed to do?

"Anything but lie. A man is supposed to stand up for who he is."

If I had told the truth, they would-a punished me worse.

"How can it be worse than it is? You're suspended for five days, and your old
man is going to beat you."

Beat me?

"I've exhausted all other options, don't you think? If I don't beat you, next thing
you know you'll be smoking dope and joining gangs and having sex with prosti-
tutes."

My hands are clutching like crazy and I want them to stop because it is not
cool to be scared of a beating. Anyway, I'm speechless when he pulls into the driveway. My mom and the two daughters he abandoned when he abandoned me at six
and the youngest one, the son of my stepfather who my mom is about to divorce,
are waiting in the yard with the front door open, and he shoves me past them without saying nothing, except for my littlest sister, his favorite, who gets her usual hug.
When my mother stops him, he already has his belt off and looped around his wrist
and he says to her, "I know this is not my house and I do not live here, but this is
my son. Please give me a room so I can beat him in private."

"That's fine by me. Give it to him good," says my mother, which is not what I
had expected her to say. Where's all that stuff she be talking about all the time?
Nobody's gonna lay their hands on my children but me. My mom says, "Use his
room," and points him to my own bedroom. For real.

And now I'm in the room with the door locked, I'm down on my knees against
the bed in which I stash my joints, and he says, "Take off the baggy pants."

Please, dad. I won't lie no more.

"I can't be sure. Take those boxers off, too."

Please, dad.

"I want you to feel the same pain and embarrassment I felt today."

Dad, what if I told you where I went today when I skipped?

"You can tell me if you want, but frankly, I don't think I want to know."

What if we talk man to man straight up? No more lies, I say.

He don't answer, just groans his no. I can't think what else to tell him. I'm running out of words. He's gonna hit me. Maybe I should hit him back. No. I only weigh a hundred and seven pounds. I gotta talk fast. The belt is in his hand.

I say to him, we'll have that special relationship again and everything.

"I don't think so, son."

Please.

"No."

But I'm your son!

They come in threes. The first three bite holes in the skin. The next three multiply the pain, and I scream so my mother who I know is listening outside the door can come in and stop this crazy shit. The third three—after he's stopped a little bit to catch his breath and I taste my own tears on the knuckles of my fist and swear that I'm gonna punch him if he hits me again—the third three land in a fresh place and I jump to my feet, screaming at him, Enough!

He pushes me down easy with his free hand and says, "You don't want me to hit your balls by accident. Keep still!"

The final three land somewhere, I don't know, which is not even the point because I'm sobbing into my hands for real and wondering why he hates me so, why he don't understand me, why no one understands me, why people just want to go abandoning me and beating me and not believing me and it's not even my fault that I got too many detentions on my record and now a suspension too, which means I'll never amount to nothing and never go to college because black crayons from an inner city crayon box got to be exceptional to be accepted, and I ain't no exception.

Maybe I should join that gang.

Maybe I should tell Curity I'm getting some from his woman and let him kill me.

Maybe I should kill myself.

Then my dad falls to his knees beside me and I'm thinking, what is this crazy shit? What's he crying for?

His arm drops around me and pulls me into his sneezy cologne space. He's all sobbing, "You're my son. I love you. I'd do anything for you. I'd give my life for you. I know how hard the world is going to be, and I worry the way you're going you won't be prepared. People are going to judge you by a lot of things you can't control. But there are things you can control if you would just try. When I see that look on your face . . . Maybe you need help. And where is your father when you need help? Where is he—?"

He breaks off into crying for real into my ear which he's soaked with eye water and slobber and his tie is crumpled up all silky and smooth under my chin, and I watch my arm snake around his neck and feel myself turn halfway into him for one of those half hugs, and it's just like back in the car again when I had no control.

I feel the trembling where our chests touch. I feel his heart beating fast under his wet shirt. I hear myself like in someone else's voice say, don't cry, don't cry, dad. Mom's listening outside the door.

He kinda whispers, kinda coughs, "She always was nosy. I'll compose myself."

Compose yourself, dad.

"I will."

And the shift in his weight means it's time for him to go, but now I don't want him to. I want him to live here again, which is not even the point because he's got a new family with a new son who does exceptionally well in school to go home to, and I know this and I'm cool with it because in my mind he's already left the room and it's already night and I'm alone in here again smoking a joint thinking about tomorrow—tomorrow when I'm suspended, and Curity's girl calls.

Or I call her.

And when I creep over to her house and get all up into her and Curity comes home from work unexpected, which is not even the point because you know he will, you know that's the only way this can end, so compose yourself, dad, don't cry—but when Curity with his badass temper mashes into little, unmoving me with this look on my face I was born with and nobody likes, I want to remember our embrace so I have something to compare it with. I want to know which one I liked better, which one was really me.

I want to know if surly was all I was.

THIRTY FINGERS

I never really wanted to play the piano, but it seemed that even before I touched my first key I could.

When the old kindergarten teacher left to go have her baby, the new teacher made us sing: "Row, row, row your boat gently down the stream . . ."

"Elwyn," said the new teacher whose long name I could never remember, "Why aren't you singing with us? Don't you know the words?"

Yes, I knew the words—just like I knew the words to "Mary Had a Little Lamb" and "Twinkle, Twinkle, Little Star"—I had memorized them as soon as the old teacher, Mrs. Jones, had sung them to us the first time. But I could not sing the words. Mrs. Jones knew why I could not sing the words but not this new teacher.

"Elwyn, why won't you sing with us?"

I could not lie, but neither was I strong enough in the Lord to tell the teacher with the long name that singing secular music was a sin. So I evaded. I said, "Mrs. Jones plays the piano when we sing." I pointed to the piano.

The new teacher said, "But I can't play the piano. Won't you sing without the piano?"

I was amazed. I had assumed all adults could do a simple thing like play the piano. "I'll show you how to play it," I said, crossing the room with jubilant feet.

"Can you play the piano, Elwyn?"

"Yes." Though I had never touched a piano key before, I had carefully observed Mrs. Jones at school and many of the ministers of music at church, and had developed a theory about playing I was anxious to test: high notes go up, and low notes go down.

After a few tries, I was playing the melody with one finger. "See? Like this," I said. My theory was correct.

The other kids squealed excitement. "Let me play. Let me play," each cried.

"What's the big deal?" I said. The high notes went up, low notes down. It only made sense.

But the new teacher had to give each one a turn. I directed them: "Up, up, now down, down. No. Up, up more."

When it came to be my turn again, I played "Mary Had a Little Lamb." The new teacher got the others to sing the tune as I played. I had but a child's understanding of God's Grace. I reasoned that if I sang secular words, I'd go to hell, but I had no qualms about playing the music while others sang.

I was young.

That day should have been the last time I played the piano, because, in truth, my fascination with the instrument did not extend further than my theory of high and low tones, which I had sufficiently proven. No, I did not seek to be a piano player. I assumed, most innocently, that I already was. Should I ever be called upon to play a tune, I would simply "pick it out" one note at a time. This was not to say, however, that I was not interested in music.

On the contrary, music was extremely important. Demons, I was certain, frolicked in my room after the lights were turned off. At night, I watched, stricken with fear, as the headlights of passing automobiles cast frighteningly animated shadows on the walls of my room. Only God, who I believed loved my singing voice, could protect me from the wickedness lurking in the dark. Thus, I sang all of God's favorite tunes—hummed when I didn't know the words—in order to earn his protection. When I ran out of hymns to sing, I made up my own.

I am your child, God I am your child—
It is real, real dark, but I am your child.

God, I believed, was partial to high-pitched, mournful tunes with simple, direct messages. God was a brooder.

What did I know about His Grace?

What did I know about anything?

〔〕〔〕〔〕〔〕〔〕

Ambition. Envy. Lust. Which was my sin?

I did not want my neighbor's wife. I did not want his servant. I did not want his ass. There was, however, a girl. Peachie. Brother and Sister Gregory's eldest daughter.

I had known her all of my life, but when she walked to the front of the church that Easter Sunday, sat down at the piano, and played "Were You There When They Crucified My Lord?"—my third-grade heart began to know envy and desire.

Peachie Gregory did not pick out tunes on the piano. No, she played with all of her fingers—those on the left hand too. Such virtuosity for a girl no older than I. And the applause!

That was what I wanted. I wanted to go before the congregation and lead them in song, but all I could do was play with one finger. I must learn to play like Peachie.

An earnest desire to serve the church as a minister of music, then, did not compel me to press my parents, a maid and a school bus driver, for piano lessons— though that is what I claimed. When they said they could not afford piano lessons much less a piano, I told them a necessary fiction.

"Angels flew down from heaven. They played harps, and they wanted me to join them. They pointed to a piano. I trembled because I knew I couldn't play the piano." I opened my eyes as wide as possible so as to seem scared and innocent. "I have never taken any lessons."

"Were you asleep?" my father said. One large hand clutched my shoulder. The other pushed his blue cap further up on his head, exposing his bald spot. "Was it a dream?"

Before I could answer, my mother said, "He already told you he was wide awake. It was a vision. God is speaking to the child."

"You know how kids are," said my father, from whose pocket the money would come. "Elwyn's been wanting to play piano so bad, he begins to hear God and see visions. It could be a trick of the Devil."

My mother shook a finger at my father. "Elwyn should have been taking piano lessons a long time ago. He is special. God speaks to animals and children. Elwyn doesn't lie."

My father's grip weakened. "But if it's a dream, maybe we need to interpret it. We can't be so literal with everything."

"Interpret nothing." The maid pursued the school bus driver to the far side of the room. He fell into his overstuffed recliner where it was customary for him to accept defeat. "You call yourself a Christian," she said, "but you'd rather spend money at the track than on your own boy. Some Christian you are."

I agreed with my mother. A child's piano lessons should come before a nasty vice. My father was beaten. He did, however, achieve a small measure of revenge. Instead of giving up his day at the track, he told my grandmother, that great old-time saint, about my "visions," and my grandmother, weeping and raising holy hands, told Pastor, and Pastor wrote my name on the Prayer Sheet.

How I cringed each week as Pastor read to the congregation, "And pray that God sends brother Elwyn a piano to practice on." I believed that God would send one indeed—plummeting from heaven like a meteor, crashing through the roof of the Church of Our Blessed Redeemer Who Walked Upon the Waters to land right on my head.

I had lied—"Liars shall have their part in the Lake of Fire."

I prayed, "Heavenly Father, I lied to them, Lord, but I'm just a child. Cast me not into the pit where the worm dieth not."

Thank God for Brother Morrisohn and his ultra-white false teeth. If he hadn't stood up and bought that piano for me, I would have surely died just like Ananias and Sapphira—struck down before the doors of the church for telling lies.

Brother Morrisohn was a great saint, a retired attorney who gave copiously of his time and energy—as well as his money—to The Church of Our Blessed Redeemer Who Walked Upon the Waters. It was his money that erected the five great walls of the church, his money through the Grace of God that brought us warmth in the winter and coolness in the hot Miami summers. It was his money that paid Pastor's salary in the Seventies when the Holy Rollers built a church practically on our back lot and lured the weaker members of the flock away. After the fire that destroyed the Rollers' chapel, it was Brother Morrisohn's money that purchased the back lot property back from the bank, putting the Rollers out of business for good.

"I can't sit by and watch God's work go undone," he always said.

On the day they delivered the secondhand, upright piano, he told me, "You're going to be a great man of God, Elwyn." He extended his forefingers like pistols and rattled a few keys: C, F#, C, F#, C, C, F#, C. Grinning, he showed his much-too-white false teeth. "I love music, but I never learned to play. Maybe someday you'll teach me." He was seventy-eight at the time.

"I will," I said. I was eight.

"I wish you would teach him, Elwyn," said Sister Morrisohn, the fair-skinned wife who was about half Brother Morrisohn's age. She removed her shawl and draped it over his shoulders and smoothed it onto his frame with her palms. "We have that big piano at home that no one ever plays."

Brother Morrisohn frowned at the shawl. "I'm not cold," he said, but he did not remove the lacy shawl. He rattled the keys again: C, F#, C.

"I'll teach you piano, Brother Morrisohn," I said.

He patted my head. "Thank you, Elwyn."

I was so happy. I hadn't had my first lesson yet, but I sat down on the wobbly stool and made some kind of music on that piano. At about two in the morning my father emerged from the bedroom and drove me to bed.

"Good night, good night, good night," he sang, accentuating each beat with a playful open-palm slap to my rump. It was a victory for him too. Just that weekend he had won $300 at the track. It didn't seem to bother him that my mother had demanded and gotten half of the money and set it aside for my piano lessons.

Every night I offered a prayer of thanksgiving, certain God had forgiven me.

〔〕〔〕〔〕

Peachie Gregory was another thing entirely.

Peachie Gregory—with those spidery limbs and those bushy brows that met in the center of her forehead and that pouting mouth full of silver braces—I didn't completely understand it when I first saw her play the piano, but I wanted her almost as much as I envied her talent.

She dominated my thoughts when I was awake, and in time I began seeing her in my progressively worsening dreams—real dreams, not made-up visions. Then I began manipulating my thoughts to ensure that my dreams would include her. At my lowest, I dreamt about her without benefit of sleep.

By age thirteen, I knew I was bound for Hell.

I couldn't turn to my parents, so one Sunday I went to the rest room to speak with Brother Morrisohn.

He said, "Have you prayed over the matter?"

"Yes," I said, "but the Lord hasn't answered yet."

He smiled, showing those incredible teeth. "Maybe He has and you just don't understand His answer. I'm sure He's leaving it up to you." The great saint put an arm around me and drew me near. He smelled of mint and talcum powder.

"Leaving it up to me?"

We stood inside the combination men's washroom and lounge his money had built. Four stand-up stalls and four sit-down stalls lined one wall. A row of sinks lined another. In the center of the room, five plush chairs formed a semicircle around a floor-model color television. We were between services, so a football game was airing. Rams versus Cowboys. Otherwise, the television would have picked up the closed-circuit feed, and broadcast the service to the Faithful who found it necessary to be near the facilities. At eighty-three, Brother Morrisohn attended most services by way of the television in the men's washroom and lounge. His Bible and hymnal rested in one of the chairs.

He said, "I don't care what anyone tells you, God gets upset when we turn to him for everything. Sometimes we've got to take responsibility. Elwyn, it's your mind and your hand, and you must learn to control them. Otherwise, why don't you just blame God for every sin you commit. God made you kill. God made you steal. God made you play with yourself."

Brother Morrisohn was so close I thought he was going to kiss me. There were those teeth again. That grin. His arm pressed hard against my ribs. But he was right. I had to control my own hands.

Brother Morrisohn began to tremble. He released me and coughed a red glob into his hand. "Age," he said with embarrassment. "Old age."

I turned on the faucet so that he could wash his hands.

I said, "What about the dreams?"

"Dreams?"

"The nasty dreams about . . . Peachie."

Brother Morrisohn rubbed his hands together under the running water. "God," he said, "controls the dreams. They're not your fault."

"OK."

"Control your hands."

"I will."

Brother Morrisohn turned off the water. "Peachie Gregory, huh?" He pointed to the television. "That was Peachie last Sunday backing up Sister McGowan's boy."

"Yes."

"She's talented. She and that Barry McGowan make a great team. He can really sing."

Barry was not my favorite brother in the Lord. Barry was a show-off, and he had flirted with Peachie in the past, even though he was five years older than Peachie and me. But now I smiled because soon he would be out of the way. "Barry just got a scholarship to Bible College," I announced.

"Good for him. He's truly blessed. But that Peachie is a cute girl, isn't she?" He laughed mischievously. "If you're dreaming about her, Elwyn, by all means enjoy the dreams."

I handed him a towel. He was a great saint.

⏐⏐⏐⏐⏐

Praise be to God, as I grew in age, I grew in wisdom and in grace. With His righteous sword I was able to control my carnal side.

While she lived often in my waking thoughts, it was only occasionally that I dreamt about Peachie anymore, and even less frequently were the dreams indecent. Awake, I marveled at how, through the Grace of God, I was able to control my mind and my hand.

At sixteen, I counted Peachie as one of my best friends and sisters in the Lord. We served as youth ministers together. We went out into the field together to witness to lost souls. As a pianist, she demonstrated a style that reflected her classical training. Disdaining my own classical training (we both had Sister McGowan for piano teacher), I relied on my ear to interpret music. Thus, on first and third Sundays, she was minister of music for the stately adult choir; on second and fourth Sundays, I played for the more upbeat youth choir. As different as our tastes were, we emulated each other's style. I'd steal a chord change from her. She'd borrow one of my riffs. We practiced often together.

By the Grace of God, genuine affection, if however guarded, had replaced the envy and lust I felt for Peachie as a child.

Thus, when Brother Morrisohn passed, it was my best friend Peachie I called for support.

"They want me to play," I said.

"You should. He was very close to you."

"But my style may not be appropriate. When I get emotional, my music becomes too raucous."

"Do you think it really matters?"

I tried to read Peachie's words. For the past few weeks she had grown cranky, and I had chastised her more than once for her sarcasm, which bordered on meanness.

"Yes," I said. "I think it matters. It's the funeral of a man I loved dearly."

"Well don't look to me to bail you out. Play what's in the book."

"I hate playing that way."

"Then play like you know how to play. Play for the widow. Play for Brother Morrisohn. Play like you have thirty fingers."

"OK," I said. "I hope the choir can keep up."

"We can," she said.

Then we talked about what songs I would play and in what order and some other mundane things, and then somehow Peachie ended up saying, "Don't worry, Elwyn. The Lord will see that you do fine. And I'll be there watching you, too."

"Bless His name," I said.
"Glory be to God," she said.

So it was a funeral, but you wouldn't know it from my playing.

Keep up, choir, I thought. I'm syncopating. Keep up!

I played for the stout old ladies of the Missionary Society, who sat as Brother Morrisohn's next of kin because at eighty-six, he had outlived most of his near relations. All that was left were his wife Elaine Morrisohn—who was now exactly half his age—and a daughter from a previous marriage, Beverly, who was a few years older than her stepmother. In their black dresses and big, black church hats with silk ribbons tied into bows, the twenty or so women of the Missionary Society took up the first two rows. My grandmother stood among them, raising holy hands. Back in the old days, when the church was just getting started, Brother Morrisohn and my grandmother, my mother's mother, had founded the group, which later became the fulcrum of the church's social activity.

Sister Morrisohn, his fair-skinned widow, sat weeping among her dark sisters. She was the youngest member of the Missionary Society and that mostly because she had been his wife. It was rumored that Sister Morrisohn had lived a life of singular wickedness before meeting and marrying Brother Morrisohn.

Beverly Morrisohn, his daughter, was not in attendance—although I had spotted her briefly at the final night of his wake. She wasn't much to look at, a round-faced woman with her hair done up in a bun. A nonbeliever, Beverly had worn pants to her own father's wake. No wonder Beverly and Sister Morrisohn hadn't been on speaking terms for longer than the sixteen years I had been alive.

I played to comfort his widow.

Watch out, ushers. I'm going to make them shake today. I'm going to make them faint. Watch out!

I played so that they would remember Brother Morrisohn, benefactor and friend. Brother Morrisohn, the great saint, who had put the Church of Our Blessed Redeemer Who Walked Upon the Waters on the map.

My fingers burned over the keys. Remember him for the pews and the stained glass windows! Remember him for the nursery!

Remember him for the piano he bought me!

Now the tilting hats of the women of the Missionary Society were my target. I aimed my cannon, fired. Musical shrapnel exploded in the air. They jerked back and forth, euphoric. They raised their sodden handkerchiefs toward heaven and praised the Holy Spirit, but it was I who lured them into shouts of dominant seventh—Hear That Old Time Gospel Roar Like A Lion!—I who made them slap their ample breasts through black cotton lace.

Remember Brother Morrisohn. Remember!

The choir was swaying like grass in a measured breeze as I caught the eye of

Peachie Gregory, my secret love, singing lead soprano. Though I seldom dreamt
about her anymore, I would marry her one day. Peachie winked at me and then
hammered the air with her fist. It was a signal. Play like you know how to play!

I did. I hit notes that were loud. I hit notes that didn't fit. Then I pulled the
musical rug out from under them. No piano. No piano—except a strident chord on
the third beat of each measure backed by whatever bass cluster I pounded with my
left hand.

Peachie gave me a thumbs up. I had them really going now.

Laying into that final chorus like I had thirty fingers, I joined them again. I
was playing for Peachie now. She kept hammering the air. I kept touching glory on
the keys. The celestial echo reverberated. The whole church moved in organized
frenzy—the Holy Spirit moving throughout the earth.

I was so good that day. Even Peachie had to admit how good I was.

Was that my sin? Pride?

⬚⬚⬚⬚⬚

At graveside, I hurled a white rose into the hole. The flower of my remem-
brance slid off the smooth surface of the casket and disappeared into the space
between the casket and the red-and-black walls of earth. The widow collapsed
beside me. I caught hold of her before she hit the ground. My skinny arms and the
meaty black arms of the Missionary Society steadied Sister Morrisohn on her feet
again. She was not a heavy woman. She smelled of blossoms sweeter than that of
the rose she held in her hand.

"I don't want him to go," she said.

"The Lord taketh the best, Sister," my grandmother said. "He lived way beyond
his threescore and ten."

"Amen" and "Yes, Lord" went up from the assemblage.

"His life was a blessing to all," said Pastor, just beyond the circle of Missionary
Society women that surrounded Sister Morrisohn.

"Yes, but I don't want him to go," the widow said.

"Throw the rose, child," my grandmother said.

My grandmother, that great old-time saint, had one arm across the widow's
back, massaging her. My own arm had somehow gotten trapped around her waist. I
couldn't snake it out of there without causing a disturbance as my grandmother's
bell of a stomach had pressed the hand flat against Sister Morrisohn. Peachie Gregory watched it all from the other side of the hole.

"Throw the rose."

Sister Morrisohn clutched the rose to her chest. "Can I see him one more
time?"

"You shouldn't, child," said my grandmother.

Sister Morrisohn said, "Please," and the August wind blew aside her veil, revealing her ears, each of which was twice pierced—before she had accepted the Lord, of course. "Please."

My grandmother pulled away, muttering sweetly to herself, "Lord, Lord," and then crunched through the gravel in her flat-soled funeral slippers to Pastor. In a loud, conspiratorial whisper, she told him to open the casket one more time.

"Amen" and "Yes, Lord" went up from the assemblage again.

When the groundskeeper, a burly man with a patch over one eye, arrived to pull the levers that raised the coffin up from the hole, Sister Morrisohn took my hand and walked me over to the edge of the shiny box in which Brother Morrisohn lay. He had an expression on his face like a man dreaming about childhood.

Sister Morrisohn fixed his dead fingers around the white rose. When she stepped back from the box, I stepped with her.

"Thas' all?" said the man with the patch over his eye. A hand in a dirty work glove rested against the controls. "Ya'll finish?"

"Yes," said my grandmother. "You may lower it again."

The man snorted, "Church folk." As he set to work lowering the casket, he mouthed what may have been obscene words but we couldn't hear him for the singing:

> *We are marching to Zion. Beautiful, beautiful Zion,*
> *We are marching upward to Zion, that beautiful city of God.*

I ushered Sister Morrisohn into the hearse already loaded with sisters from the Missionary Society. "Thank you, Elwyn," she said, squeezing my hand. "He really cared about you. Your music meant so much to him."

"Thank you. I'm glad."

I remained by the door because she yet held my hand. I could not command her to release it; she was the widow. Should I tell her that Peachie Gregory was waiting for me, that we had planned to stop off at Char Hut to finish our grieving over french fries and milkshakes? How does one break away from the recently bereaved? I averted my eyes and in a sudden move wrenched my hand from her grasp.

When I dared look again, the hand that had held mine was brushing at tears.

"Don't forget about me, Elwyn."

"I won't," I said.

Strange music began to play in my head. Was it the aroma of her flowery perfume making me light-headed? I could still feel the shape of her waist in my empty palm. She was not a heavy woman. God forgive me, I silently prayed, This is Brother Morrisohn's widow. Brother Morrisohn, a man I loved.

When I got to my car, where Peachie awaited, I was breathing as though I'd just run a great distance.

"The church is going to be a sadder place without Brother Morrisohn," I said.

"Poorer," Peachie answered, as we drove to Char Hut. Her forehead was beaded in perspiration despite the wind from the open window that animated her long braids. It was hot, and my old Mazda had no air conditioning. "No more free rides for the Faithful. The candyman is gone."

"At any rate," I said, "I think we presented him a great tribute."

"Especially your playing, Brother Elwyn. It brought tears."

I ignored her sarcasm. "He was a great saint. He'll be missed. I for one am going to miss him."

"You and the widow both."

"What?"

"Nothing." Peachie stared out her window. She would not look at me. "I said nothing. Nothing," she said.

She was not telling the truth—she had indeed said something, a something that unabashedly implied impropriety: "You and the widow both." I may have been in love with Peachie, but I was not going to suffer her insolence. I had never been anything but a gentleman with any of the sisters at the church, Peachie and Sister Morrisohn included. How dare she intimate such a vile idea! Such a rude side of Peachie I had never encountered.

Was Peachie jealous?

Just as I was about to chastise Peachie for her un-Christlike behavior, my old Mazda stalled.

"This old car," she muttered.

"God will give us grace," I said, cranking the engine to no avail. The Mazda rolled to a stop in the middle of traffic. Other cars began blowing their horns, whizzing around us.

I got out. Peachie crawled into the driver's seat. I popped the hood and jiggled the wire connecting the alternator to the battery. Peachie clicked the ignition at regular intervals. When her click matched my jiggle, the frayed end of the wire sparked in my hand and the engine came to life. I closed the hood, got back into the car. "That takes care of that."

Peachie stared out the open window again. "I'm not hungry. Take me home."

"Peachie—"

"Please, just take me home."

I passed to the center lane to make a U-turn. The traffic light caught me. I floored the clutch and the gas pedals so that the car wouldn't stall while we waited for green. "You could at least tell me what I did to upset you."

"Who said you upset me? I have serious things on my mind."

Serious things I little doubted. She was jealous.

"Ever since you got into the car, you've been answering me curtly or ignoring me altogether. I thought we were friends." The light changed. I made the U-turn. "See there," I said, "You can't even look at me."

"Says who?" She turned on me with angry eyes.

"Are you jealous of Sister Morrisohn?"

"Jealous of the fragile widow?"

"Are you jealous?"

"Now you're being silly." Peachie laughed. "Wait. Are *you* in love with Sister Morrisohn? You certainly seemed concerned about her at the funeral. And what—do you think she's in love with you? She's only about ten times your age."

"Ouch. You don't have to be so mean to me. I just thought that maybe you felt threatened."

Peachie looked at me with eyes that mocked. "And what—how can I feel threatened? Do you think, my dear brother in the Lord, that I possess any feelings for you other than the sincerest and purest friendship?" If she had been standing, Peachie's hands would have been akimbo. "Did I forget to share with you that Barry McGowan has written to me several times from Bible College?"

"Barry McGowan?" Why didn't he just leave her alone? At twenty-one, he was much too old for her. "What does Barry have to do with this?"

"He graduates in December. He's building a church up there in Anderson, Indiana. He already has the land and everything. He wants me to direct the choir." Then she added with finality, "He wants me to marry him."

"What? Well you won't," I said. "At least you won't marry him now. You still have school to finish. And your mom and dad—"

"They're all for it," Peachie said. "They love Barry. And I can finish school up in Anderson, and then go to Bible College."

"But they'll just let you go like that? You're so young."

"Lots of sisters get married young," she said, as though I should know this. And well I should, having played at many of their extemporaneous weddings. But Peachie didn't have to go that way. She was virtuous, I was sure. "Don't worry, Elwyn, Barry can take care of me. He's a great man of God."

I had trouble focusing on the road. "No, no, no. This is so sudden."

"I've been thinking about it for four months."

"Come on, Peachie, stop kidding around. Four months! You never told me."

"I know."

"We're best friends. You tell me everything."

"Everything but this." Her features softened, and she lowered her eyes. "I didn't tell you this, Elwyn—because, I guess, I didn't want you to hold it against me. You're so perfect, so holy."

"I'm not that holy. I told you that I deceived my parents in order to take piano lessons."

"That's small, Elwyn. Everyone does little things like that," she said. "I took piano lessons with Sister McGowan in order to be around Barry."

"You never told me that. You're making this all up."

"Elwyn, you're so innocent, you wouldn't understand how these things happen. If I had told you about Barry and me, you'd have held it against me."

"I'd never hold anything against you." I said a silent prayer for courage, and the

Lord sent me courage. "How can I hold anything against you, Peachie? I love you."

"Don't say that."

"But I do. I love you—"

"Elwyn, do you?"

"—and I think you love me too, Peachie."

"Why didn't you tell me this before?"

"You knew. We both knew."

"Oh, Elwyn."

I let go of the gearshift and found her hand. "Don't go to Anderson with Barry. Stay here with me. You are the love of my life. You are the only girl I will ever love."

She squeezed my hand in both of hers for one hope-filled moment. Then she pushed it away.

"Stay, Peachie."

Peachie shook her head. "I can't."

"You can," I said.

Peachie patted her stomach. I had to look twice before I understood. Now it made sense, but impossible sense.

"You and Barry?"

"Four months."

"But that's a sin. Fornication. The Bible says—"

"It is better to marry than to burn."

"But you have defiled your body—the Temple of God."

"God forgives seventy times seven. Will you forgive just once, Elwyn?"

How could she smile such a cruel smile? She was mocking me. And the church. Where was her shame? I wanted to cry, really cry. My Peachie, whom I had never kissed. Gone. Out of the ark of safety.

"Christ is married to the backslider. Barry and I went before God on our knees. We repented of our sin. But you, Elwyn, will you forgive us?"

"I'm not God. It's not for me to forgive."

"It's important to me. You are my true friend."

"I'm not God."

She made a sound somewhere between a gasp and a sigh. My Mazda stalled again. I got out, walked around to the front, and popped the hood. I jiggled as Peachie clicked. Oh God, I prayed, give me grace.

〳〳〳〳〳

I didn't feel so holy as I waited for the last remnants of the Missionary Society to leave Sister Morrisohn's house.

My grandmother, of course, was the last to go. She stood on the porch with her heavy arm draped over Sister Morrisohn's shoulder telling the grieving widow some last important something. As my grandmother talked, she scanned the surroundings. East to west. What was she looking for? Did she think I would make my move with everyone watching? She should have known that I would park down the street behind a neighbor's overgrown shrubbery where I could see and not be seen.

My grandmother embraced Sister Morrisohn and kissed her goodbye on the cheek. At last, she lumbered down the short steps with the help of Sister McGowan, the mother of Barry, who often gave her rides now that she was too old to drive. As Sister McGowan's car pulled off the property, I fired up my engine.

I left my black funeral jacket and tie in the car. I prayed for courage. I rang her doorbell.

"Elwyn. Come in."

"Yes ma'am."

"Sit down. Would you like something to drink? I've got fruit punch."

"OK."

I was sucked into the plush red velvet couch. Mounted on the wall across from me was a large oil painting of them on their wedding day. She was chubbier as a young woman. He looked about the same. Beneath the painting was the grand piano he had bid me play every time I visited his house. I remembered that two years prior, we had performed our Christmas cantata right here in their living room. I had played "O Holy Night," while Barry, on Christmas break from Bible College, had sung. I had foolishly thought that Peachie's enthusiastic applause was meant for me.

Sister Morrisohn, still wearing black, returned with a glass of fruit punch and a napkin. I took it from her and she sat down on the couch a few inches away from me. I drank the better part of my punch in one swallow.

She cupped her stomach. "I don't know when my appetite will return. I haven't eaten but a mouthful of food since I woke up and found him. I knew it would come one day, but I still wasn't ready for it. We're never ready for it, are we?"

"Well," I said because I didn't know what else to say. "Well."

"If it weren't for the church, I don't know how I would have made it. Everyone has been so nice to me."

In a voice that flaked from my throat, I said, "You must have loved him."

"Yes. I was a very different person when we met. He saved me from myself. He led me to the Lord."

She was different when he met her. I prayed, Lord forgive me, as I glanced at her doubly pierced ears. What was she like before? Could she be that different person again?

"Before you met him, what kind of sins did you commit?"

"Sins? I don't think about them anymore." She raised holy hands. "Praise God, I'm free."

"Praise God," I said, raising holy hands, careful not to spill the remainder of my drink. "But are you ever tempted?"

"All are tempted, Elwyn, but only the yielding is sin." She clapped her hands. "Hallelujah."

"Hallelujah," died on my lips as my eyes followed her neck line down to the top button of her blouse. Bright flesh showed through the black lace like a beacon. All the signs were there, her smell, her touch, her plea that I not forget her. I would not let her get away as Peachie had. "But do you ever feel like yielding?"

"What?"

I folded my napkin under my glass of punch and with trembling hand set the glass on the octagonal coffee table before the couch. I turned and reached for her hand.

"Elwyn?" she said. "What are you doing?"

I kissed her on the mouth. I pressed her hands up against my chest. She pulled away from me and sprang to her feet.

"Elwyn—Help me Jesus!—what are you doing?"

"You're a beautiful woman," I squeaked, but it was no use. She was not to be seduced.

"Elwyn!"

I buried my head in my hands.

"You need prayer, Elwyn," she said. "You need the Lord."

"Yes," I said, without looking up. "Yes."

Now there was a soothing hand on my neck—like a mother's. I wept and I wept.

"Serving the Lord at your age is not easy, Elwyn. Don't give up." Sister Morrisohn rubbed my neck and prayed. "Christ is married to the backslider. Confess your secret sins."

And confess I did.

And then I wept some more because the more she rubbed my neck, the more forgiveness I needed. For when she got down on her knees beside me and began to pray against my face, the very scent of her expanded my lungs like a bellows, and her breathing—her warm breath against my cheeks, my ear, into my eyes burning hot with tears—was everything I imagined a lover's kiss would be.

My Father's Business

At sixteen, I met my first great temptation, and I yielded with surprisingly little resistance, I who had proclaimed myself strong in the Lord. There had been, it seems, a chink in my armor, and Satan had thrust his wicked sword through it.

As I wondered how I could have felt so strong and yet been so weak, I labored mightily to get back into the ark of safety.

I took a more active role in the Lord's work. On Sundays, I rose early and joined the maintenance Brethren in preparing the main hall for morning service; I stayed late to help them clean up afterwards. Brother Al and Brother Kitchener were surprised but happy to work with me. Often, we discussed music.

"Elwyn, I really like when you do that dum-dum-da-dum thing at the end of service," said Brother Kitchener, a retired seaman of about seventy who had both a stoop and a limp. When he pushed a broom, he resembled a man perpetually about to play shuffleboard.

Brother Al, a squat man with a massive chest and arms like telephone poles, shouted down from the ladder upon which he stood replacing a cylinder of fluorescent light: "I was first trumpet in my high-school band."

Unemployed and in his late twenties, Brother Al spent his days lifting weights or visiting the three children he had sired out of wedlock with a Nicaraguan seamstress named Bettie. This was, of course, before he had accepted the Lord.

"Maybe you and me'll do a duet one Sunday," Brother Al said.

"Maybe we will, Brother," I said, scraping chewing gum from the bottom of a pew with a butter knife.

Now on those Sundays when it was not my turn to play piano for the youth choir, I stood as usher at the entrance to the church: *I'd rather be an usher in the house of the Lord than a prince in the palace of hell.* My legs, standing motionless for the better part of the hour, were diligent for the Lord, my knees strong and true.

I stopped the children from talking or fighting, tapped them awake when they fell asleep. "Suffer the little Children to come unto Me," Christ says. When babies cried, I was quick to pull them from their grateful mothers' arms and take them outside into the calming sunlight, or lead some other mother—a visitor—to the rest room at the back where she could change a soiled diaper, or perhaps nurse her baby.

When the Holy Spirit descended, I waited for Him to touch one of His favorites—Sisters Davis, Breedlove, Naylor, or Hutchenson—and set her to trembling, to move upon her so powerfully, in fact, that she would collapse. I would rush to the fallen sister and drop the large velvet shawl over her spasming legs, hiding what would otherwise be revealed—the usher is the guardian of decency—and then with the help of another usher, I would carry the fallen sister to the nursery where she could rest on a cot until the Spirit had passed.

Scripture says it is not through our works that we are saved; only through His

Grace. And Scripture can't be challenged. But, I reasoned, after the Devil had
caused me to offend the widow, that if I were indeed going to work, let it be in the
service of the Lord.

It struck me that part of my problem was that I didn't pray enough; yes, morning, noon, and evening found me on my knees, head bowed, but what about the
times in between? Scripture does admonish us to pray without ceasing. So I
increased my standard prayers to five times a day, and I began a campaign of fasting
on the weekends.

One Sunday afternoon, during the lull between morning service and youth
hour, I sat in my bedroom reading from the Book of Daniel, searching perhaps for
my own handwriting on the wall. I heard my grandmother say:

"Elwyn's not eating today?"

As was customary, we had guests over for Sunday dinner—my grandmother
and Sister McGowan, my old piano teacher.

My mother answered, "Elwyn's fasting."

"Fasting?" I heard my grandmother say. "Every time I come over here he's fasting."

My mother said, "All of us Christians should be fasting along with Elwyn.
There is so much trouble in the world."

"Especially the way them Arabs have shot up the gas prices," said my father.

"Please pass the salt," said Sister McGowan.

"Here it is, sister," said my father. "Over there in the Middle East, there's sure
to be a war. Armageddon."

"We are living in the last days," said my mother.

"Watch and see if the Lord doesn't return soon," said my grandmother.
"Watch and see." There was a chorus of Amens, and then she continued, "I still
think he's been too serious lately. Something's bothering him."

My mother said: "Know ye not that I must be about my Father's business?
The Lord was only twelve when he said that."

My grandmother's voice boomed. "Don't quote scripture with me, girl."

"Mother," said my mother, timidly.

"I know my grandson. And I know—"

"So much salt?" I heard my father say.

Sister McGowan answered, "I know it's bad for my blood pressure, but I've had
more of a taste for it since Barry and Peachie announced they're getting married."

Oh Peachie. My foggy eyes could not read the prophet. I found my ear moving
closer to the open door. Why did I want to hear what I already knew?

"Peachie and Barry make a nice couple," said my father. "I pray their children
don't witness Armageddon.

"They're so talented," said my mother.

Then there was awkward laughter as they attempted to maintain the pleasant air.

"Humph," snorted my grandmother, "All this time I thought she was Elwyn's girl."

"Mother," said my mother, "Elwyn doesn't have a girl."

"At sixteen?" said my grandmother.

"But he likes girls, I can tell you." My father laughed without vigor. "He's my son."

"I-thought-Elwyn-liked-Peachie," my grandmother said, punching each word. It became quiet.

I pictured my grandmother, her large arms folded across her chest, her head tilted at a defiant angle, and everyone else seeming to eat but only just touching their lips with empty forks, or filling their mouths with drink they did not swallow. My grandmother was an old-time saint. She wielded the truth like the two-edged sword Saint Paul says it is. She was noted for rebuking the women of the Church of Our Blessed Redeemer Who Walked Upon the Waters when in the late Fifties they thought it was acceptable to straighten their hair. Later when the skirt-like *gauchos* became popular, my grandmother exhorted the women not to wear them because skirt-like or not, *gauchos* are pants, and women weren't supposed to wear pants.

It was about a half minute before my grandmother's voice broke the silence: "But now I guess Peachie and Barry have to do what's best."

"I've seen them . . . they do love each other," said Sister McGowan, the mother of Barry, the father of Peachie's unborn child.

I felt a useless anger well up in me. This anger was an emotion I, the meek, forgiving Christian, was unused to. Anger obscured the obvious: Peachie was lost; and the other one, the one I had harmed, the widow, should never be mine. I prayed for a clear head.

"It's probably Elwyn's fault," my grandmother said. "He's too serious for these modern girls, that's what."

"He tries to be a good Christian," my mother said.

"I guess you can't blame him," said my grandmother. "But he could at least give me a hug. He played so nice today."

"Yes, he did," my mother said.

"Lord, I'm proud of that boy," my grandmother said.

"He was always my best student," Sister McGowan said.

"The actual city of Armageddon," said my father, "is somewhere in the Middle East, isn't it?"

Forks clinked against the good china again, and my stomach growled. I sipped from my glass of water, which was the only thing the Faithful were allowed to consume on a fast. Lord, give me strength, I prayed, and I headed out to the dining room and greeted Sister McGowan and gave my grandmother her hug.

Fasting left me numb, light-headed, closer to God. Fasting was good. Before it was all over, I had fasted four consecutive weekends. A month of hungry weekends.

I was trying to be about my Father's business.

At my high school, I did not speak to my acquaintances except to witness to them. Admittedly, a large number of students fled at the sight of me. Others hungrily accepted the tracts and Bibles I handed out. There was always a crowd at the prayer meetings I held in the back of the cafeteria during lunch. Many came to laugh and deride, but others bowed their heads and uttered their first timid words to their creator. More than a few shed tears.

I skipped classes in order to confront those of my fellows who were themselves skipping to smoke marijuana cigarettes and vent their carnality in the dark dressing chambers between the band room and the auditorium. These last were not happy to see me, but as God was on my side, they came to respect, both spiritually and literally, the power of the light I brought to them. None could escape the Faithful servant of God.

I was on the battlefield for my Lord.

In fact, I increased my evangelistic efforts so much so that I found myself barely paying attention at school.

I was busy saving lost souls—John Feinstein; Eldridge Pomerantz; Marco Japonte; Marigold Hendricks; the bubbly Anderson twins, Tina and Sabina; and many more to whom I was spiritual leader. What did I care about trigonometry?

I ended up sitting on a backless chair in the principal's office.

Mr. Byrd was a short man with a voice that thundered. His office was dominated by a large, wooden desk overflowing with pink and yellow sheets of paper. In a wooden picture frame nailed to the wall directly behind the desk, was a color photograph of Mr. Byrd and a plump woman wearing a pair of riding pants and riding boots. The woman stood a few inches taller than Mr. Byrd, who had his arm around her waist.

"Just stop it," Mr. Byrd said. He sat on the edge of his desk, an unlit pipe hanging out of his mouth. "Stop it."

"I am a child of God," I said.

"Amen. I'm a deacon. A Baptist," he said. "But I'll expel you if you don't stop it."

"Then you understand, Brother Deacon," I said, "I've got to do my Father's business."

"Just stop it." His heavy voice seemed to shake the walls.

"No, sir."

"Would you like me to call your parents?"

"They support my evangelism."

"That's right. You're all fanatics. That whole Church of the Blessed Christ Walking Whatever-you-call-its."

I was prepared for such as he. "The Faithful is what we are called. Feel free to make fun of us because we don't drink, don't smoke, and our women don't wear pants."

"Pants?" Cupping the bowl of his pipe in his hand, he turned and glanced at the picture on the wall of him and the woman in the riding pants. "What's wrong with pants?"

"Pants," I said. "Deuteronomy 22:5. A woman shall not wear that which pertaineth unto a man."

"What a strange lot. And you don't danceth, or weareth jewelry either?" he mocked.

"We do not."

"King David danced. He wore a good deal of jewelry, too."

"David was before Christ's time. That's Old Testament."

"Deuteronomy is Old Testament, too," he said.

"Well, Christ didn't do away with everything under the old law."

"Not those things which please your church, at any rate." Mr. Byrd hopped off the desk. He raised the volume of his already incredible voice. "They didn't even have pants in the Old Testament!"

I was undaunted. "A woman shall not wear that which pertaineth unto a man." But my time was too precious to argue with Mr. Byrd. I should be out serving the Lord. "I guess Baptists can do just about any old thing they please."

"Don't mistake us for you." When Mr. Byrd laughed, the unlit pipe whistled. He opened a folder filled with pink sheets of paper and read: "Six unexcused absences, seven tardies, failing English, failing health, a warning in trigonometry—do you plan to go to college, Elwyn?"

"Yes. Bible College."

Mr. Byrd sighed, as though I, a child of the King, were a lost cause. "Do you plan to graduate high school?"

"Of course."

"Then stop it. Get back to being the student you were."

"God's will."

Mr. Byrd closed the folder. "I don't want to expel you, Elwyn. You're not the worst kid we have here."

He signaled with his hand for me to leave, and I stood up.

"Just stop it."

I shook my head. "No, sir."

"The Bible is a book about life here on earth, Elwyn. For your own sake, start living life."

"I am living, deacon. But perhaps you'd rather I smoked a marijuana cigarette or got someone's daughter in trouble."

"You wouldn't know where to start," he said.

I opened the door and stepped out of his office. "Praise the Lord," I said.

Mr. Byrd's door slammed behind me.

I was gracious with Barry McGowan. I even shook his hand in brotherhood during one of his trips home from Bible College to preach a sermon on humility. Barry proved a charismatic speaker. That and the two songs he performed evoked thunder claps of "Amen" and "Yes, Lord" from the congregation in spite of what he had done. I wished Barry well and meant it.

I also wished Peachie well, now that her condition had become obvious and the congregation was reacting to her as it always did to those who had strayed. Pastor had removed her from the choir and relieved her of her duties as minister of music. She no longer led prayers at youth hour, though she continued to give a cautionary testimony that moved all of us teenagers to avoid lasciviousness and be stronger Christians. Like me, Peachie was determined to regain that special relationship with God which she had lost.

I asked Peachie and Barry if there were anything at all I could do.

"Play the organ at our wedding," said Peachie.

"I'd be honored to, Peachie." I embraced her, careful not to disturb the unborn child, who seemed to kick, she said, especially hard when I was around.

Barry said, "Remember, Elwyn, this is a wedding. None of that boogie-woogie stuff you like to play." Barry was a tall man, broad with thick limbs, whose little head seemed wrong for his Goliath body. When Barry shook his head back and forth, it reminded me of those wobble-headed dogs people decorated their dashboards with.

"Don't be silly, Barry," said Peachie standing between us, holding one of my hands, one of his. "Elwyn's always done a fine job at weddings."

"I'm just making sure. Things are bad enough as it is without the musician going boogie-woogie on us."

"Things aren't that bad," said Peachie, who was five months pregnant.

"I'm just making sure," Barry said. "I'm not flexible on this point."

"I promise I won't play boogie-woogie at your wedding, Brother McGowan," I said, smiling up at him. "Especially since I don't play boogie-woogie. It's called gospel."

Peachie shot me a warning look, but Barry didn't seem to take notice or offense. "Well that's settled," he said, nodding his little head. "Now how much is it going to cost? You know we're on a tight budget with me trying to build the church up in Anderson and all."

Before I could even answer, the groom-to-be had said, "We'll pay you twenty dollars. If you want more than that, my mother will get one of her students to play." He glared at me with his little eyes. "I'm not flexible on this point, Elwyn."

Sister McGowan, Barry's mom, wouldn't play at a wedding for less than $350. My usual fee was $100. But—Praise God—the Holy Spirit bridled my tongue.

"Barry," I said, "there's no charge. Think of my music as a wedding gift."

As Barry struggled to figure out how I was getting one over on him, his eyes grew large in his little head. "A gift?"

"Thanks, Elwyn," Peachie said. She gave me another hug and then flinched. "Ugh. The baby just kicked. Isn't that funny? Every time you're around, Elwyn."

Barry shook my hand. "Thanks a lot, Brother Elwyn. And no boogie-woogie, right? I'm still the groom."

"Anything you say, Barry. Praise the Lord."

I had asked God for grace, wisdom, humility, and strength. And He had given them to me. A little more than a month after my transgression and already I had gotten over Peachie. I had stomached Barry, even Barry. My faith was stronger than it had ever been. I was well on my way to becoming a great man of God, a beacon unto the Faithful.

Now there was but one thing I had left undone, my confession, and with my renewed faith I was willing even to do that.

Of late, I had ceased avoiding the widow's eyes. I had greeted her quite pleasantly one Sunday as I stood usher and she passed through the doorway amid a trio of Missionary Society sisters. I had addressed her by her name, Sister Morrisohn, and cast a friendly smile her way. She had seemed surprised, but smiled back, waved with her fingers. Is this the same Elwyn who had offended me so foul?

Yes, I was he, that vile, weak creature, but now I had thrown off my mantle of iniquity and been reborn. Christ lived in me.

Yes, if the widow so desired, I would even confess my secret sin.

Peachie married Barry the second Saturday in October, and all of the congregation was there. The members of the bridal party were Peachie's thirteen-year-old sister Gwen, who stood as maid of honor; Ricardo, Brother Al's four-year-old Nicaraguan son, who was cute and precocious as the ring bearer (we all laughed when he loudly echoed the "I do's" of the bride and groom); and Brother Philip, Barry's roommate from Bible College, who stood as best man.

Peachie wore a powder-blue dress that was tailored to hide the obvious. O, she was beautiful, my Peachie, despite the somewhat desolate expression she wore throughout the ceremony. Then again, who could be truly happy marrying Barry?

At his own wedding, Barry sang a solo, "O Perfect Love," which drew tremendous applause. He sang on his knees, troubadour style, looking up at Peachie. His mother accompanied him on piano while I sat at my silent organ musing. They hadn't told me about the solo, and it wasn't in the program.

Barry and Peachie's reception was the first gathering held in the church's dining hall since we had renamed it three Sundays ago the Buford Morrisohn Dining Tabernacle in honor of our late benefactor. The Faithful ate home-baked pastries and drank grape juice beneath pink and blue wedding streamers and Brother Morrisohn memorabilia: the photographs of him from childhood to adulthood, the plaques we had given him over the years, his degrees from Tuskeegee and Oberlin, even his birth certificate. He had been our greatest saint.

He had been my friend. It was he who had purchased the old upright that stood in the hallway of our home, the piano upon which I had learned to play.

I had no appetite. In my mind, the Buford Morrisohn Dining Tabernacle that afternoon was divided into three zones. Peachie and Barry controlled the middle zone, surrounded by food, drink, well-wishers, levity. I occupied the zone at a far end, away from the commotion. At the other remote zone sat the widow. She seemed more interested in the pictures of her late husband than the newlyweds. She still grieved, as did I.

I passed through the throng of well-wishers gathered around the bride and groom—"Congratulations, Peachie. Good Luck, Barry, though I know you won't need it, ha, ha, ha"—and made my way to Sister Morrisohn's side of the room.

"Hello."

"Elwyn!"

"I have to tell you how sorry I am," I said, getting right to the point.

"For what?" She closed her eyes, then opened them slowly, remembering. "For that? Don't let it worry you."

"What I did to you . . . what I assumed about you was horrible."

"Did I strike you as that kind of a woman?"

"No, it was all my fault. I was confused. Forgive me."

"I forgive you."

"Thanks for forgiving me."

"God, I'm sure, has already forgiven you, and that's what really counts."

"Praise His name."

"I hear," she said, "about all the things you're doing around the church and at school. You're amazing."

"Praise His name," I said.

"And this. I don't think I could have played at Barry's wedding if I were in your place."

"It was just a wedding."

"Don't deceive yourself, Elwyn." She extended her hand, and I helped her out of her seat. "All liars, even those who deceive but themselves, shall have their part in the Lake of Fire."

I took my hands away from her and shoved them in my pockets. A few feet away Barry guided Peachie's hand as she cut their cake. A camera flashed. There was applause. It all seemed very far away, as if happening in another country but being broadcast on TV.

"Peachie and I never promised each other anything."

"Deception, deception."

"No, really."

"It must have really hurt you. She reached up and touched the side of my face near my mouth with her fingers. "Poor boy," she said. "Love is often cruel.""

I considered Sister Morrisohn's own mouth, the way the bottom lip poked out when she pronounced a word with an open vowel sound: "You," "Poor," "Boy."

The Devil was causing me to focus on the pink on that pulsating bottom lip, and urging the physical manifestations of lust to appear on me. I reminded myself that I was strong in the Lord. Strong! I reminded myself that I was still in control of my feet.

"Sister Morrisohn, I've got to go." I got me away from her and walked straight to my car. In a blur of confusion and emotion, I sped down familiar streets made unfamiliar by my anger at my shameful weakness. Fearing what I might do to myself, I pulled over to the side of the road, clasped my hands, and bowed my head before the steering wheel.

Lord, I prayed, give me a sign. Show me what to do.

My vision cleared. I looked up and saw that I had parked beside a canal. A large turtle rested in the grass on the shoulder of the canal. I got out of my car. I picked up a long branch that still had some leaves on it and prodded the turtle with the branch until it retreated into its shell. I put down the branch and pondered the large turtle safe inside its shell and at length concluded that if this were, in fact, a sign, then I certainly had no idea what it meant.

At about 6 p.m., when I figured the reception had ended, I drove back to church to help the maintenance Brethren clean up.

I would work for the Lord. I would be strong. Praise ye Lord!

I was the last one to leave the church that night. And when I left, not a scrap of dirt remained.

The next day was Sunday, and I fasted.

Sunday night, I received a call. I recognized Peachie's voice, but she was crying so much that it took me a few minutes to figure out what exactly she was saying: "I made a mistake, and now everyone hates me."

"No one hates you, Peachie. And you know God loves you. His greatest gift is that He forgives us our sins."

"It's not that, Elwyn. It's just that everyone thinks I deceived you."

I sat up in my bed. "What?"

"Your grandmother makes it sound like I—"

"My grandmother?" Of course. The truth is like a two-edged sword. It cuts going and coming.

"Sister Morrisohn, too, and that whole Missionary Society. They make it sound as though I—"

"Sister Morrisohn?"

"Yes, she wouldn't even talk to me at my own wedding."

Peachie deteriorated into sobs and it was a while before I could understand her again.

"Sister Morrisohn is who pressured Pastor to kick me off the choir."

"But you're pregnant," I said. "What do you expect?"

"It has nothing to do with my pregnancy!" Peachie shouted. "There've been pregnant girls up there before and you know it. You said yourself God has forgiven me. They wouldn't even let me have a regular wedding. That ugly blue dress! The real problem is I offended their pet. You."

"Me?"

"With all the witnessing and stuff you're doing at school, you make the Church of Our Blessed Redeemer Who Walked Upon the Waters look good. All of those new converts. And me, your perfect mate, big and pregnant for another man."

"That's not how it is," I said.

"That's what it looks like."

I felt a great sadness for Peachie and her plight, but in many ways this turn of events served her right. These were the wages of her sin, the fact that she had wronged me notwithstanding. I could not tell her this, so I tried to change the subject.

"Where's Barry?"

"He's right here. He told me to call," Peachie said. "He's afraid they won't ordain him if I don't apologize to you."

"Peachie, this is ridiculous. You don't owe me any apologies."

"Yes, I do."

"No, Peachie."

"I'm sorry, Elwyn. I'm sorry, Elwyn. I am so very, very sorry," she said. "I hope that satisfies you, you arrogant knucklehead."

"Oh Peachie, don't be that way."

The second day after Peachie married Barry was a Monday, but I did not drive directly home from school.

I stopped by Mr. Byrd's office. I was a conqueror come to claim a new country for the Lord.

With an exasperated expression on his face, Mr. Byrd looked up from a folder whose contents he had been studying. "What now, young evangelist?"

"I feel I'm being persecuted for my religious beliefs."

"How so?"

"Security broke up my prayer meeting today."

"Good," he said. "I sent them." He closed the folder and came around the desk. "The cafeteria, I believe, is a place for eating. Many of the students complain that your activities upset their stomachs so much that they can't eat their meals."

"I don't believe you. What students have complained, sir?"

"Don't press me, boy."

I had him where I wanted him. I opened my book bag, pulled out five sheets of paper. "I have a petition here signed by over a hundred students and staff who feel that we should be allowed to form a Jesus Club at this school—."

He snatched the papers from my grasp. "I don't see my signature," he said. "I am the principal." He tore the petition into eighths and sprinkled it into the wastepaper basket.

"I have a photocopy," I said.

"Who cares? The real issue is not your prayer meeting but your grades. This is a school, not a church."

We stood toe to toe now, and he proved to be about a half inch shorter than I (and I am no giant), but I was suddenly afraid of him. I shrank at the sound of his deep, angry voice.

"I know Christians, but you're not one, Elwyn. You're weak. And you use your religion to shield your weakness. You can't make it on the football team, so you lure the best players away to your Bible studies."

"I'm not an athlete. They come freely."

"You can't get a girl, so you preach about adultery and fornication."

"Fornication is ruining our women."

"Not my woman. And I got a woman," he said. He pointed to the photograph behind his desk. "A big, happy, sexy woman. Look at her smile."

"I'm happy for you."

"You should try passing your classes instead of passing out Bibles."

"I can pass if I want to. I'm an honors student."

"You were an honors student. What happened to you?"

"I'm smart."

"Smart enough for Bible College at any rate. What SAT scores does Bible College require?"

"What is that supposed to mean?" I was on the verge of tears, and I didn't know why. "You're persecuting me."

He grabbed me by the shoulders. "Don't use God as an excuse for failure and unhappiness, Elwyn. Don't think that your misery on earth is a free ticket to heaven. Have fun. Be young. Pass your classes."

"No!" I could not prevent the tears from rolling down my cheeks. Satan was winning. Then whack. Whack. Whack. Mr. Byrd slapped me three times hard in the face.

With the tip of my tongue, I tested my lip, which had begun to swell. It stung like a revelation. I stared without anger at little Mr. Byrd.

"Now you'll probably sue me for assault," he said as he ushered me out of his office, one hand behind his back holding the door open against its strong spring.

I did not drive directly home after getting slapped by my principal. I visited Sister Morrisohn. A Christian must be valiant, brave.

"I am saved."

"By the Grace of God."

"How, then, did I let go of His unfailing hand?"

She forced my hands together. "Pray, Elwyn."

I bowed my head and closed my eyes. A sobering thought prevented me from praying, and I opened my eyes. "You never told anyone what I did that day."

"There was no point in ruining your reputation. A good name is rather to be chosen."

"I would have lost my position in the church, like Peachie."

"You didn't really sin," Sister Morrisohn said. "Peachie sinned."

"I did sin."

"But you prayed for forgiveness."

"So did Peachie. And she confessed openly. I didn't so much as do that. Open confession is good for the soul."

"God knows the heart. That's enough, don't you think? Let your little transgression be a secret between me, you, and God."

"But the secret is driving me crazy." I was at a crossroads of faith. I either had to do what the Bible said was right, or not do what was right at all. It was now 4:15. Sister Morrisohn wore a red sundress. A half hour ago she had removed her shoes. I had been here almost an hour. I had told her the Devil had got a hold of me and made me love her, and she had removed her shoes. Another revelation. She had beautiful feet.

"There are many secrets in the church. Those who confess are no worse than the rest, but they suffer for their forthrightness."

"The Bible says open confession is good for the soul."

"Everyone will treat you like a backslider. You don't want that." She closed her eyes. "Some will even laugh at you."

"Laugh?"

"You're so much younger than me. They would find that amusing."

"Did they find it amusing," I asked, "when you married Brother Morrisohn?"

This seemed to catch her off guard. Her face underwent a series of quiet transformations, from disbelief to anger to resignation, before she spoke again: "How old are you, Elwyn? Sixteen?"

I nodded.

"That makes me twenty-seven years older than you." She rose from the couch where she had been sitting for about the last half hour, and she walked in her stockinged feet to the other side of the room. She stood under the portrait in oil of her and Brother Morrisohn on their wedding day. It was a painting in broad strokes and drab colors: black, gray, a rusty brown, a pasty yellow where white should have been. "I was married for twenty years to a man over forty years my senior. I loved him every second of that marriage."

"You're saying it doesn't really matter, then, the age difference."

"It matters little. Oh, there are times when it matters." She laughed suddenly into her hands. "I just can't believe that at your age—well, just look at me." Sister Morrisohn lifted her arms like wings and spun in gay circles, revealing herself from all sides.

I gazed unabashedly. She had dancer's calves, a slender waist, arms that were thin as a young girl's.

"I see nothing wrong with you."

"Look at me again." Now she grabbed her hem with both hands and raised it above her dimpled knees. "All of these imperfections that come with age." She spun. Her sundress spread out like an umbrella, exposing thigh-high garters and the black silk panties of mourning.

When I looked at my watch, it was 8 p.m.

"Elwyn, this is a secret you'd better keep." Sister Morrisohn rolled over and buried her face in my chest. She laughed, and then she cried.

I cried.

What pieces of our clothes we could find, we put back on, and then we knelt at the foot of the bed. But she was too close to me, and Satan won the battle again. My hand went under her dress and touched her there.

"Oh, God," I said.

"Lord," she said.

And then we sinned again—me and the woman who smelled like spring blossoms, whose slender waist had fit so pleasingly into my palm, the woman who did not weigh much when she fell. Me and the wife of my deceased benefactor and friend.

Afterwards, she said, her cheek against my neck, "How are we going to do this, Elwyn? People may begin to wonder."

"I could be giving you piano lessons twice a week," I suggested.

"Good," she said. Then: "Only twice a week?"

I called home once more.

"I'm still at the mall," I said to my mother. "Witnessing."

"Don't forget dinner is waiting for you," she said. "Or are you fasting again?"

"I'll be home in a while. I'm hungry. My fast is over."

"I'll keep your plate warm. Bye, Elwyn."

"Bye, Mom."

Father, forgive me.

The C-Plus Baptist Virgin

WHEN I DROVE MY CAR through the plate glass door of Albrecht's Bookstore, I ruined $200 worth of adult magazines. I was speeding, I was drunk, and even though my net worth amounted to whatever my rusted Honda was worth in spare parts minus what I owed for insurance late charges, I was represented in court by Marcus Tishman, Esquire. In America, every case has two sides, mine being just as valid as that of the old lady of tomes, Dame Wilhemina Albrecht herself.

The way my legal counsel and I saw it, Dame Wilhemina had neglected to place a lighted sign in plain view in front of her store informing midnight motorists, such as I was, that parking was in the rear and not inside the store as it is in many of the fashionable bookstores in New York and San Francisco. Our novel defense failed, of course, but I got to say my piece before the people of Lake City, Florida, and especially Dame Wilhemina, who could buy me perhaps a million times over. I laughed defiantly in open court.

"Tell the pompous rich that this is America, where all men and women are created equal!" I said, wagging a finger, as the stenographer recorded my every word. Court was cool. America was cool. Thomas Jefferson was cool, though a bit crude in his reasoning to grant me the same rights as my hardworking parents, whose money I frittered away on kegs, comic books, and changing majors. Alas, the joke was on me.

Dame Wilhemina, for instance, asked me to spend my one hundred hours of community service sweeping her parking lot and unloading boxes of heavy law textbooks; and I, though disdaining manual labor, agreed to the work because we, the Dame and I, were in fact not equal. She chaired the Board of Regents of my junior college, and I enjoyed being a college student, which gave me a kind of celebrity status among the local church folk, whose pretty daughters, their foreheads scorched by hot combs, their uneven teeth, their broad hips, pushed me (husband material!) to the very edge of my chastity. When I proved such an efficient law textbook unloader so that by the third day I had little else to do but chat idly with Mikolos, the wheelchair-bound head cashier who collected X-Men and Green Lantern, Dame Wilhemina informed me that she also owned a 500-acre horse ranch that needed an extra hand.

"I wouldn't know what to do on a horse ranch," I said.

"You'll learn to use a shovel and a wheelbarrow," said the old lady, her face powdered and stately.

"It's nearly summer. I'll die of heat stroke."

"Wear white, Mr. Johnson." The woman owned me.

Each day I found an area about the size and shape of a football field marked off with pink flags. I pushed the wheelbarrow over the thickly matted clover and, depending on the size and degree of decomposition, collected horse dung with a scoop or a shovel. At the end of about an hour when the wheelbarrow was full, I pushed it to one of the four huge compost heaps back of the main barn and emptied it. Then I pushed it back to the marked-off area and set to my task again.

I'm not certain what lesson all this was supposed to teach me, a good-natured black youth from a mixed suburb, but you wouldn't believe how much dung the Dame's forty horses produced. She called them jolly, playful, and proud, these beasts that roamed her property as unguarded and unfettered as their feral kin. In fact, they ate oats from her frail hand. If I came near them, however, they exploded into violent motion. I must scurry up a tree or be run over. Then, with malicious kicks, they'd upturn my wheelbarrow and spill its contents onto the ground. Later when I set to my task of re-shoveling what they had upturned, they'd stand a few meters away to watch. Their spirited neighing could be easily mistaken for laughter. If all men are created equal, I reasoned, these horses should like me. I shouldn't have to collect dung.

It was Dame Wilhemina's granddaughter Helga who explained it to me after I had shoveled for the day and sat drinking ice water with her under the ivy-choked eaves. "And you call yourself a history major," she said.

"I switched, last week, to English."

"Even worse," she exclaimed. "The answer is in the syntax, Mr. Johnson!"

"What do you mean?" The ice water was as refreshing as the vision of Helga lying propped up on her side in a reclined lawn chair. She was dressed in all white, too—a bikini top, baggy shorts, sandals.

"Don't you see?" said Helga, the philosopher queen, her ivory skin darkening in the sun. "The forefathers employed the passive voice. 'All men are created equal,' but created by whom? Transpose this to the active voice, and you get 'Someone created all men equal.' Can you guess who this mysterious creator is?"

"Quite obviously it's God, which anyone can deduce without having first to shuffle the syntax," said I.

"You're missing the point," she said, frowning. "Thus transposed, the statement reads 'God created all men equal,' or rather, 'equally,' which you must admit doesn't explain who we are so much as how we came to be. God didn't create each of us the same; He created each of us the same way."

I was a Baptist. In responding, I was careful not to blaspheme. "You make it sound as though the founding fathers make a statement of religious faith rather than a call to genuine brotherhood."

"Indeed they do, Mr. Johnson!" Helga sat up suddenly, spilling a good bit of the water across her freckled chest. She leveled the half-empty glass at me. "Their phrasing clearly implies a working-class god, churning us out in his celestial factory. Chunk-clink. A human. Chunk-clink. A human. Chunk-clink. Another human." The monster horses galloped in the background.

"God is not a factory worker, Helga."

"God is not anything," she said. "But don't miss my point. God expends as much effort to make crippled Mikolos as He does to make me or you."

Helga did not hide the fact that she was an atheist. Still, in my heart, I shoveled dung for her alone. I had but twenty hours of community service left. After that, I would see her only on the chance that she entered her grandmother's bookstore on a day I happened to be there discussing comic books with Mikolos—which, of course, would be every day.

"It's a free country," I said.

Helga made a farting sound with her lips. "Each of us has a station in life, a pattern bestowed upon us at birth, constraints that are social, physical—"

"We're equal. Anyone can do anything he or she wants."

"I would like to see Danny DeVito out-jumping Michael Jordan."

I laughed it away. "A horrible example. Then again, if DeVito applied himself, who knows?"

"B.S."

"The point is no one will stop him from trying."

"I'd like to see poor Mikolos dance."

"Now, you're being mean."

"My point is still my point."

"Mikolos is the nicest person I know."

"Forget Mikolos." She sounded exasperated. "I'll settle for you standing up to my grandmother. A brilliant man doing such brutish labor."

"I am brilliant. I am a man."

She raised her fist. "Power to the people. Revolt."

It was a Sunday afternoon. I looked beyond Helga to the area I had cleared that morning. Dame Wilhemina, in a full-length, white gown and a tricornered, lace-trimmed hat, played croquet with her dear friends, the mayor of Lake City and his wife. A black serving woman in a leather vest and riding boots helped the Dame swing her mallet. The final distinguished guest, the president of my junior college, sat in the grass watching them. He sipped a drink. He had loosened his tie and removed his shoes. He was thinking, perhaps, of joining the game.

"Revolt," said Helga.

"Not today," I said, momentarily humbled in the presence of my betters. "I have a paper to write."

"B.S.," she purred. "You are so equal it hurts."

But I was telling the truth.

At any rate, the bourbon party my roommate threw didn't disturb my writing nearly as much as I thought it would, because fortunately I had figured out most of the essay in my head while shoveling. In fact, the bourbon balls I chugged pretty much obscured the smell of horse dung so I could concentrate on grammar and word choice. I woke up the next morning cotton-mouthed but with a neatly typed paper. It was simply amazing how well I performed under pressure. Then walking into the classroom, I chanced to spy the new grade, C+, posted next to my student code, J55755, on the door where Professor Walton publicly charted the class curve.

This had to be a mistake, or perhaps the horse fumes had confounded my senses. I peered more closely and drew a line from student code to grade list with my finger. Yes, the first C was my summary of dry *Don Juan*, which I had Cliff's-noted through. And this, the C- on flaky Blake, this could have been at least a B, but Professor Walton had assigned it during the NCAA Final Four. And following these was that new and unassuming C+, which wasn't a bad grade to be honest, but I hadn't earned it. Hell, the essay was still in my hand, or had I turned one in last Wednesday when it was originally due and then forgotten about it?

I marched in with the others and endured fifty minutes of Shelley and Thackeray, and Professor Walton rising on the balls of his feet to shout, "The trumpet of prophecy! O, wind, if winter comes, can spring be far behind?" I was an English major, so I wrote it down. Then, sobered up somewhat by lecture's end, I decided a good Baptist must be honest. I met Professor Walton at the doorway.

"What is it, Johnson?"

"About my midterm paper, sir."

He glanced at his grade book. "C+, Johnson. Much better, but still room for improvement."

"But Professor—"

"You know how I feel about students who question their grades," said Professor Walton, staring down through bifocal tints, his steel-gray ponytail hanging off his shoulder like a pet serpent. He was cool during the Sixties.

"But how can I get a grade if I didn't turn in my midterm in the first place?"

"Are you sure?"

"See?" I pulled out my essay. "See, here it is." I passed the four stapled pages into a hand that had black fingernails on the thumb and forefinger.

"Yes," he said, holding it up to his face. He leafed quickly through it. "Yes." He whipped a pen from his breast pocket and marked the last page, all the while humming to himself. "Here," he said, handing it back.

I looked down at a C+.

"This is unfair. First, you give me a grade for a paper I didn't even hand in—"

"I'd call that a lucky break. Had I noticed your paper was missing, I'd have given you an F." The tall, skinny man turned away from me. I pulled him back.

"—then when I do turn it in, all you do is skim it."

"Let go of me. Calm down."

"I'm going to the dean."

"Because you disagree with my grading system?"

"You have no system." I folded my arms across my chest. I owned him and he knew it, and now he would have to buy my silence. An A in British Literature would be a nice padder for my new major. And it was not like my paper was so bad. "Life and Death in the 'Ancient Mariner'" had taken three hours to type. I had experienced visions, not unlike Coleridge's, by the compost heaps at Dame Wilhemina's. Feces was my opium. What is life but an interruption of eternal death? For an eternity we are nothing, then for seventy or eighty years we are something, then for an eternity again, nothing. Deep stuff. I had used big words, too.

"I guess now I'll have to read the damned thing." He snatched the paper from my hands and this time took about six minutes to get through it, grumbling, his red pen looping and swirling. In the end, he said: "It's really just a C, Johnson. Your grammar, as always, is atrocious. How refreshing it would be if you employed a verb that's not in the 'to be' family. I'm giving you the C+ because your content is stronger than average. Amusing. Coleridge as a faith healer. You could use more supporting detail, however."

"This is B.S.," I announced to the gathering crowd. "I'm reporting you, Professor Walton. Something's got to be done about teachers like you." I waved the paper above my head. If Helga could see me now.

"Teachers like me. You might remember that I am, in fact, your teacher."

"You're a fraud!"

"Is that how you see it, Johnson?"

"Yes."

"Perhaps we should talk in my office."

"It won't do you any good," I shouted. "Power to the people!"

"Lower your voice," he said, leading the way down the hall.

Maybe I wasn't equal to Professor Walton, but his felony, academic dishonesty, was less than equal to my misdemeanor, common sophomoric slothfulness. I would do to him what the Dame was doing to me. In fact, if he offered money, yes, I'd take it. It was about time the good guys won one.

Then he opened his door.

His office was a clutter-free room with bright sunlight bursting through jalousies painted green. There were no papers on the desk, no over-stuffed folders lying around, only about ten reference-type books on the shelf behind the desk alongside his potted plants: gladiolas, miniature fern, and a vine flowering red that crept up the back wall. Dominating his broad desk was an immense computer alongside its companion laser printer. I wondered at the letters "S-P-A-G" embossed on both machines in fancy script.

Sitting down at the computer, which was already turned on and whirring, Professor Walton said, "I'm no fraud." He punched up some figures, and my name in bright green poured across the screen, a grid, a graph, a pie chart, and a column of numbers calibrated to the hundredths following it. "This is how I grade papers, Johnson. At the beginning of the term, I grade two of your essays by hand and scan them into S.P.A.G. along with some personal information. Your GPA, your age, years in school, SAT's, hobbies, how much alcohol you consume in a month, religion, whether or not you're a virgin, how late you stay awake at night, favorite sports team—"

I recognized the information as what I'd answered on a questionnaire he'd passed out the first day of class.

"—and then S.P.A.G., or Student Profile Analysis Grader, does the rest. I tell S.P.A.G. the assignment, and it predicts how you will perform."

"Based entirely on my past performance?"

"And your tendencies," he said. "It predicts performance."

I winced at my hopeless scholastic profile unspooling across the verdant screen. "In other words, this machine guessed at how I would have written this paper based on the fact that I'm a black, sophomore, compulsive drinking, Southern Baptist— well, OK!—virgin?"

"You're over simplifying the process," he said, "but basically you're right."

In high school I had earned A's and B's without studying. I was better than this. "This is wrong. Unfair. A pigeonhole of the worst kind," I said.

"Revolutionary is what it is." He tapped the print command and offered me a smile that can only be described as sinister. The printer came to life, whistling, and he handed me the four gleaming pages it spit out. I gasped at an essay entitled "Life and Death in the 'Ancient Mariner'" by Artemis Johnson, Jr.

"No."

"Read it, Johnson."

I read it. It was my paper, almost word for word. Actually, it was better than mine. The part about Coleridge's being a faith healer was further developed, and it included a humorous anecdote about a fishing trip my father and my pastor might have taken. Incredible. And there was that grade: C+. "This is too spooky."

"The cutting edge of technology," he said. "What a blessing S.P.A.G. is. I teach five classes per term, thirty students per class, six papers per student. S.P.A.G. allows me to devote my full energies to lecturing." He spread his arms, indicating the larger conspiracy. "There's one in every office, a gift from the Board of Regents."

"The Board of—" I shook my head no. "My English teacher doesn't read my papers."

"A strain on the eyes. Hell, even without S.P.A.G. I could predict most grades without glancing at the page." His voice became sing-song: "In this day and age of overwhelming drugs and abuse, we Americans in our society today have discovered, in my opinion, I feel, that the 'Ancient Mariner' is a very pertinent and also important poem to read because Samuel Taylor Coleridge, the author and poet who wrote the 'Ancient Mariner,' at times used drugs in his day and age when he was alive."

It was the first paragraph of my paper exactly, except mine was about death and eternity.

"I lecture," he said. "Let S.P.A.G. separate the C's from the D's."

"But, Professor—"

He put up his hands. "Yes. Yes. So I gave a grade to a student who hadn't actually done the work. I was sloppy. It won't happen again."

I pleaded, "What I'm trying to say is I won't always be a C+ writer. I can change. You're a teacher. You of all people should understand that we're not locked into patterns. We all have free will—"

"You got drunk this weekend, Johnson, didn't you? You wrote this breezy paper—which was already late—at some ungodly hour in a place less than conducive to collegiate concentration, didn't you?"

What could I say? Between 2 and 5 a.m. during a bourbon party.

He said, "Fortunately, S.P.A.G. is kinder than I am. It accounts for growth potential. The more you write, the better you'll write. By senior year, if you survive, you'll be a more serious student."

"I could change now."

"S.P.A.G. doesn't see it that way. But if you get laid—er—find a girlfriend before the term is over, tell me." He winked. "It's worth half a letter grade."

I shook my head. "Real change, professor."

"Real change? Change your parents, your sex, your faith?"

"But I might shine on any given assignment."

"You might also beat Michael Jordan in one on one!" He slapped his desk.

"It's like I'm stuck with my fate."

"That, in fact, is the working definition of 'fate.'"

I sighed at my fate in the pie chart on the screen: a hard-drinking, comic-loving, C-plus Baptist virgin. Damn. I turned to go.

Then Professor Walton cleared his throat. "One more thing, Johnson. What is that horrible smell?" He scrunched up his nose.

"Horse dung." Closing the door behind me, I heard the keyboard's tap, tap, tapping, and I counted, H. O. R. S. E. D. U. N. G, while thinking, I should change my major to astronomy, or perhaps political science. I might be real good at political science.

My last twenty hours of community service at Dame Wilhemina's ranch were the worst, as Helga was nowhere to be found. The horses forced me into the canal, and I dragged myself out soaked. But the second time, I said, what's the use? It was too hot anyway. I might as well enjoy it. I kicked off my shoes, tossed my shirt and my pants up on the banks. I swam from one side to the other, singing a happy song, until the horses went away. Dame Wilhemina found me stepping into my white pants. She did not avert her eyes. "Johnson," she said sharply, "I might remind you this is not summer camp."

"That's for sure." I turned my back to her, zipped up my fly, picked up my shirt, wrung the water out of it. "The horses tried to kill me."

She sat in the motorized cart she tooled around her property in, its engine humming. "Am I to understand that the horses stripped you down to your underwear?"

"You know full well they chase me. You've watched them do it. They're evil"—I stepped into my soggy shoes—"like you."

"Don't make me out to be the bad guy." She pointed a crooked finger. "It was you who got drunk, you who destroyed my property. I think I've been quite lenient."

I shivered into my wet shirt. "Lenient? What if I quit right now?"

"With just a few hours to go? I'd think you foolish as well as reckless." Twisting her painted lips into a smile, she raised her cell phone. "I'd have you arrested."

"Where's Helga?"

"What?" Gone was her smile. "Are you challenging me, Johnson?"

"Helga, Helga." I raised my fists above my head. Revolution. I did a little dance. And the monster horses turned toward us, thundering, their hooves unearthing clumps of grass and black soil with every angry step. I panicked. I picked up my shovel and bent to my labors. The horses veered away, playfully.

I sighed.

"What was that about my granddaughter, Mr. Johnson?"

"Nothing, Dame."

"Continue your work."

"Yes, Dame."

So lift, fall. Lift, fall. This was who I was. I lifted that shovel and brought it down hard like I was stabbing at the chink in my enemy's black armor. I worked myself to exhaustion. Back at the compost heap, the fumes got to me. I was overcome. I fell in. I was haunted by pedantic visions, man.

Jefferson said, "All men are created equal." A toothless tobacco grower from North Carolina said, "Even the poor? The poor smell bad." That started the silver wigs shaking in dissent, and Jefferson had to raise his hands to calm them. He quoted scripture: "Whatsoever ye do unto the least of My children ye do also unto Me." "Yes, but the poor don't own land," said the representative from North Carolina. "And they're stupid, or they'd be rich like us," said a banker from Pennsylvania. "If they are stupid," said Jefferson, in a desperate effort to save the union, "they won't understand their right to a gun, a bottle of apple jack, and a vote. We, on the other hand, shall have fulfilled our duty to our Lord by showing kindness to our lessers." The First Continental Congress exploded in applause. There was dancing in the aisles.

I awoke, spitting invertebrates from my mouth, and wincing from the open-palm slap of my savior, the black serving woman in the riding boots, who smacked me twice more before I stayed her hand.

"Are you OK?" She was pecan colored with smiling eyes, her hair pulled back in a bun. "For like ten minutes, you were just sitting there so still."

"I'm better now."

"Yuck. There's maggots on your cheek." She flicked my face with her fingers. "What were you doing? Were you praying or something?"

"In the compost heap? I passed out."

She beamed. "Then I saved you."

"Well—"

"But don't thank me. I'm always saving people." She took my sticky hand and rose, pulling me to my feet. "It's my gift. God guides me to those who need me most. Five years ago, I found Miss Wilhemina in the ladies room at the bookstore having a heart attack. Same thing. I didn't even have to use the bathroom, but God told me to go in there."

"Lucky for her," I said.

"Lucky for me. I've been working here ever since, and Miss Wilhemina, as you know, pays us very well."

I wiped my hands on my pants leg. "How would I know? I'm just her body servant."

She nodded her head. "At any rate, Mikolos and I are closing on our house next week."

"Mikolos? The guy in the wheel—" I began. My head was still groggy. I picked up the shovel. "—the cashier at the store? I know him."

"You do?"

"We talk comics. He never told me about you. Well, well, well, Mikolos, you devil."

She blushed. "I'm Judy."

"Artemis."

"I love comics, too. She-Hulk," Judy said. "Albrecht's has the best selection in Lake City. That's why I was in there."

"Well, well, well." I rested my weight on the shovel and gave her a sly look. "Mikolos never mentioned you."

"He's cautious," she said. "Some people are real funny about exceptions."

"No kidding," said I, the expert on exceptional romance. Helga and I, for example, were perfect for each other. She was born to a life of luxury, and I had practiced luxury all my life. But would I ever be allowed to quarter my horse in her corral? "People get used to patterns. Blacks go here, whites there. Oh, I know exactly what you mean.

"Do you?" Judy said. "How do you tell your parents that the man you're going to marry is disabled?"

"Oh."

"That they'll never have grandchildren?"

"Oh."

"The only good thing my folks will say is at least he's a Baptist."

"Oh."

"But tough. They'll get used to it," Judy said, and clenching her fists, she might have been a pecan She-Hulk. "No one is going to take away my right to pursue happiness."

"Yes," I said, all the while thinking, poor girl, poor girl.

But Helga and I did meet again, on Friday, my last day. Oblivious to my sadness, she was on the attack—inalienable rights this, democracy that. I shook the ice in her bourbon, then handed it to her. "Tell me something I don't know, Helga." I peered into eyes of gray. "If it's such a self-evident truth, why don't we cast off these imaginary chains that bind us, that separate us?"

"That's what I've been trying to tell you, Mr. Johnson. It's a religious thing, really. The self-evident truth excludes the savage Indians, because they felt they were created by a thundering bird."

"Is that right?"

"Yes," she said. "And you servile Africans—you felt yourselves brother to spiders and lions. You're excluded, too."

"Government of the people," I said. It was useless, but I was trying. "For the people, by the people—"

"But not for us women, or chattel as we were called, who must be subject to our husbands, as the church is subject to the so-called Christ."

"Now that's going too far! Aren't you afraid that when you die you'll end up in Hell?"

"Didn't you used to be a history major?" Today Helga sat with her legs crossed. She wore long white pants to hide the bruises. All week, she had been breaking a new horse, who threw her twice yesterday, only once today, as the Dame looked on unflinching, she had reported. "Jefferson was an atheist."

"Atheist? I doubt it. What I do know is he fathered a bunch of children by his slave women. His descendants are legion in Virginia."

"His most revolutionary act, Mr. Johnson. He helped them break out of their pattern. So to speak."

"So it *is* possible to break out of our pattern."

"You tricked me, Mr. Johnson."

She offered me a sip, her sunburned arm spanning the grassy void. I took the drink from her. I drank from where her lips had drunk. It was good bourbon. Southern. Expensive. We held that glass. I considered a way of breaking out of my own pattern that would teach even Dame Wilhemina a lesson. S.P.A.G., too. It was not the drink. I was sober. But Helga meant more to me than a half letter grade. I leaned into her where she sat. Put my hand around her bare midriff. Got excited when she didn't immediately push it away. Got nervous. In my shadow, her gray eyes appeared the color of bourbon.

She breathed. "You never stood up to my grandmother."

"She's got money, power," I told Helga, whose breasts were crushed against my chest. "I'd have to be certain—"

"That—?"

"—that you'd be there with me."

In the ensuing silence, Helga became darker but no less attractive. My fingertips made circles on her bare midriff. Circles on the small of her back. Helga said: "In life, Mr. Johnson, only the ugly truths are certain."

"In other words, we are not so equal as equally created."

"Poor Mikolos will never dance."

"At least he's got his comic books." I shook my head. "Hell, he's got more than that." I released the glass, which fell to the earth. I closed my hands around her. I kissed her full on the lips. I made it last for longer than ten seconds. I imagined she made a sound like "Mmm" and rolled her eyes toward Heaven. We broke for air. There was grass in her hair. Her eyes slowly opened. Her hands were locked behind my back under my shirt. Please grant me this, I prayed. I moved to kiss her again. She looked away. Began brushing her hair with her fingers. I put an arm around her. She was patient with me. Kept brushing her hair. I removed my arm.

"So you're changing your major again."

"To astronomy or political science."

She was back on her lawn chair with her legs crossed. "There's less writing in astronomy," she said.

"I'll do astronomy then." In a moment, I moved from under the shady eaves and back to my wheelbarrow in the sun. I had about another hour of horse dung to shovel, but already the revolution was over.

His Baby Momma

From the corner of his eye, Harvey Benjamin saw the safety break away from his man. This was Montgomery, who, though cross-eyed and small, delivered the hardest hits in the league. Montgomery ran with his head down, a torpedo hurtling toward Harvey's ribcage, but even he was too far away to make a difference. Up there already was the ball, falling as from the sun. Harvey's fingers formed a nest in the wind. If I catch it, we win.

The ball came filled with memories and pain.

He brushed them away, grasping.

The ball touched the heels of his hands and bounced away.

"God-damn!" he cried. "God-damn." Like this was the final play in an NFL game, and he the goat who had just blown his team's chances at playoff and glory. This was only a scrimmage in the North Miami Kumquat League, and he the goat who had just blown a keg of Pabst Blue Ribbon Beer. But God-damn. God-damn. Because his mind had flashed back to this morning when Priscilla told him she was going to marry Roderick. Today.

By now they were at the courthouse.

He should have seen it coming. This Roderick, in his bow tie and his thick glasses, was a geek who had improved himself with money. First, he had leased that Lexus. Now he had a fine woman to complete the picture. Living large. Priscilla was so young minded! But if she wanted a husband, Harvey insisted, "It should be me, the father of them twins."

"'Them twins have no father" is what Priscilla had said.

"What am I?" Harvey had pounded his chest. "What am I?"

"You don't give them any money."

"Because I ain't got no money. But when I make it to the pros, them twins'll be livin' large."

"You're twenty-eight, Harvey. Keep dreaming."

"Dreaming?"

"Your hip…"

"Ain't not a damn thing wrong with my hip."

"You limp."

Priscilla backed away when Harvey shouted "Bullshit!" and punched his fist.

Priscilla checked her tone when she said, "Well, you only come to see them when you want to be with me."

"That ain't true."

"You hate children."

"Don't say that, baby. If you hadn't-a pushed me so far…"

Priscilla, who was one of those really dark women and tall, looked away. Sometimes Harvey forgot how beautiful she was, and then she'd smile and he'd hate himself for letting her move in with Roderick. A friend at work who was just trying to help. He shoulda checked that shit right in its tracks. He shoulda checked it. But what else could he do after they had evicted him?

"I love Chaneka and Raneka," he said. Turned her around and pulled her against his chest. Long-legged, skinny girl, reaching almost as tall as him. Still warm from her bath. Kissed them fine hairs that covered her cheek and neck. Stuck his nose between her warm breasts. "Ain't nobody gon' marry my baby momma."

"Harvey, stop."

Rubbing up against her the way she likes, his fingers lifting the elastic band.

She grabbed his hand. "Harvey, I'm getting married."

"Married. Shit. I can hold you til' Roderick get back, you know I can." He controlled her with just that one arm around her waist to show his strength. He waved the other in the air to show her how easy it was. "Let me kiss you," he said. "Give me a damned kiss. You know you want to. Stop acting so young minded."

She opened her mouth. It was a good kiss. She was getting sticky down there. Bucking against him with her knees, like she does. He led her into Roderick's workroom, where the camera equipment was set up. He lay her on the day bed where she claimed she had slept before the thing with Roderick began. He took off his pants. She sighed and twisted out of her panties like he was making her do something she didn't want to do. So young minded. Kept sighing. Made him wear a condom. Her long legs up against his chest, he loved her as well as he knew how, but Priscilla was non-responsive. He knew she knew it was good. What they had was good. Trying to act like she didn't feel it. He worked it hard till she clapped her knees together. Started giving it back hard on her wedding day.

When it was over, she sat up on the edge of the bed. His head was in her lap like it used to be. She said, "Say goodbye to the twins."

"After five years? Hell no, baby!"

"I've got to get dressed."

He pounded the mattress. Then hugged her around the waist and rolled on top of her. "I love you so much. Don't you see?" He tried to position his face in her lap.

She shoved him off. "Go kiss your children."

"Priscilla."

She threw him an ugly look. Then she got up and started stepping into her underwear.

"Priscilla!"

She stood at the half opened door, buttoning her housecoat now. In the other room, the twins sang the theme from *Barney*—"I love you, you love me"—and she turned her head toward the sound. Harvey noticed her face was still irregular from the one time he had lost his temper. The one time. She said, "Next week, Roderick and I need to discuss child support with you."

"You bitch."

"Get out of my house. I swear to God I'll call the police."

He moved towards her.

"If you touch me again I swear to God I'll scream."

The twins in the other room were crying. Screaming. This was not what he wanted. "Priscilla."

"Get out, get out, get out, get out!"

So when he left Roderick's house, he was indeed unfocused. But to drop a ball when he was wide open was a source of genuine discomfort for Harvey Benjamin, who had once been invited to the Dolphins' training camp and earned four words of praise from Don Shula—"You could've been great"—before he was asked not to return.

"I am great! Don't you know I hold the Peach Bowl record? Don't you know I'm a warrior? Fast. Strong. This hip don't bother me at all," he said, as security had walked him to the gate. "I can take a hit!"

Dropping that ball was nearly as jarring as the blow cross-eyed Montgomery delivered a half second later that lifted Harvey a yard off the ground and set him down hard on the back of his neck. It knocked his wind out. It made his nostrils flare.

Everyone gathered around Harvey while Dr. Pelezo, who was really just a registered nurse, checked his blood pressure and asked him to count fingers.

"Two."

"Five," said Dr. Pelezo, holding up five fingers. "Now how many?"

"Five."

"One," said Dr. Pelezo, holding up one. He rubbed Harvey's buttocks. He slipped his fingers under the thigh pad, moved his hand up to the sensitive place on the hip, and when Harvey flinched, he said: "How do we feel?"

"Normal."

"Come on. How do we feel?" He squeezed it.

Harvey squealed, "Jheezus Christ, doc. You should a played linebacker."

"Still hurts?"

"No." Harvey held his breath. "I smell bleach, though."

"Ah, bleach," Dr. Pelezo said. "Wonderful. You need only rest."

Cross-eyed Montgomery said, "I thought I'd killed another one," and there was laughter as everyone began to clear out of Harvey's sunlight. The shadows were growing long on this last Saturday in August, and the high school marching band from whom the field was borrowed was ready to begin practice. Someone played scales on a trombone. There was the friendly tinkling of bells. Harvey pondered the cadences of a youthful drummer: Rat-a-tat. A-tat-tat-a-tat.

Bo Deckle, Harvey's roommate from back in college, helped him to the sideline and laid him on a bench in the shade of a coconut tree. Coach Red was stomping over, tearing the game plan in half. "Coach look mad," Bo observed.

"Real mad?"

"That's fo'sho'real." Bo patted Harvey on the shoulder and jogged to the locker room.

Coach Red roared: "Get up!"

"Coach, I took a bad hit."

"Get up! Get up!" Coach Red grabbed Harvey by the shoulder pads and pulled him to his feet. Harvey, feeling dizzy, reached out and grabbed hold of the big man's forearms.

"Coach…"

"What the hell're you doing out there?"

"Montgomery was breathin' down on me."

Coach's face was all deeply furrowed age lines and freckles interrupted by a nose broken too many times to count. "Three times you was wide open," he said, shaking Harvey.

"Wasn't my fault. I heard footsteps," Harvey said. "I smell bleach."

"Smell what?"

Cymbals crashed. The tubas in the high school band played the bass line of "The Star-Spangled Banner."

"Can I sit down, coach?"

"Punk. P-U-N-K. Punk in your heart! Sissy in your gut! Get that demon out of you, boy. "

"Ain't no punk, coach."

"In a pink dress and lace slippers. Cinderella with a moustache."

A few players looked on as the chewing out continued. Beyond them, Dr. Pelezo got into his Toyota pickup, headed to the grocery store for the keg of Pabst Blue Ribbon for the other team, as he was also the team accountant. When he honked his horn, Coach Red, who was in the middle of saying something about "tits on a bulldog," turned his head.

Dr. Pelezo made a sign like a man brushing away a fly. Coach Red nodded his understanding.

As Harvey pondered the silent exchange between coach and team medic, the entire high school band began to play "The Star-Spangled Banner."

Now when Coach Red turned back to Harvey, it was with a calmer voice: "I don't know what else to tell you."

"I ain't no Cinderella, coach."

"Don't you see what I'm trying to tell you?" He released Harvey, and said, "It's all Freudian. Life is football. Football is life. You can't score if you don't catch the balls. I see you out here doing this at your age, and I'm ashamed."

"I got balls, coach. I'm a producer." But really Harvey didn't understand what was going on.

"I'm cutting you from the team. Your body's kaput. Give up."

Harvey struggled to his feet. "My body's fine. My hip's fine. My mind was on some other stuff today. My girl been actin' up. But I play with pain. If you just give me another chance."

"If if, then then," Coach Red said. "If my granma had wheels, then I'd be a Cadillac."

"What?"

He put his hands up like a blessing. "Time to move on, son. Really."

"But coach, " Harvey winced, "it ain't my fault."

After his final scrimmage, Harvey stretched out on the back seat of Bo Deckle's 1980 Buick Electra 225. The back wall had thinned with rust, so he could smell the gasoline from the lawn mower clanking in the trunk. He and Bo mowed lawns on the side. He owned the lawn mower and did most of the work. Bo, lazy-assed Bo, owned the car that got them to the sites. He had his hands over his eyes to shade them from the sun so he could sleep, get away from this stupid day, rest, wake up, think what to do next, but it was impossible with Bo involving him in conversations he could scarcely decode.

". . . better chance this year than last, that's fo'sho'real."

"Don't matter to me no more. Screw the Kumquat League."

"Not us. The Dolphins, man. Marino's back. They just said on the radio he's back. Shakin' that big ol' ass."

"Marino got a big ass?"

"Shakin' so much you wonder how it don't fall out."

"Dan Marino got a big ass?"

"Marino? Yes. No. This girl we just passed, the sexy señorita in them cut-offs." Bo's marijuana perfumed the air. "She's foin, that's fo'sho'real. Foin, foin, foin as sweet sherry wine. What you wearin'?"

"Bo, leave me alone. I'm tired."

"Wearin' to Priscilla's, I mean. To her wedding."

Harvey put his head between his hands to squeeze out the ringing. He wondered if Priscilla would tell Roderick what they had done that morning. How many times she had come. Maybe he should tell Roderick. Maybe he should ask Roderick for a job. He should knock Roderick on his ass. "Priscilla got married an hour ago."

"To who?"

"The photograph man, I told you."

"When they getting married?"

"Pay attention or go to hell, Bo. Leave me alone." Harvey's hip cried pain.

"Man, I could eat me some wedding cake, watch me some pretty girls. Where's the reception?"

"Leave me alone."

"At the Portrait Studio, of course, we going. Eat me some cake. Pull off these sweats. Get a jacket or something. Big bowtie. Clean shoes and socks."

"We ain't going."

"Of course we going. Them twins gettin' a new daddy."

"Them twins already got a daddy. I'm-a kick your ass, Bo."

"How you support 'em without a job, daddy?"

"Don't go there, Bo."

"Cuttin' grass. Guess you could be a security guard. I just hope he don't whup on 'em too much. You know how stepdads is."

"Just cause I got this bad hip don't mean I won't whup *him*."

"Yes, you will. Yes. Just like you whupped Priscilla."

Harvey sprang up.

"I ain't sayin' that's why she left you. No. Yes. No woman don't stop loving her first love just cause he whup her a little. Just cause she pregnant don't mean she can't take a whuppin'…"

Harvey slapped the back of Bo's head. "I'm-a kick your natural black ass. You know damned well what happened with me and her." He slapped the back of Bo's head until the car lurched to a halt. Then leapt out and pulled open Bo's door. Put the finger against Bo's nose. He said, "If she had acted right, if she hadn't-a been so young minded, I wouldn't-a touched her." He pressed Bo's nose, daring Bo to cross that line again.

And Bo, his skin so black, smiled like a happy garden ornament, and said: "Tire flat."

"Tire?"

"Flat."

They drove the Buick off the road and into the parking lot of a shopping strip. Bo popped the trunk. Harvey hefted out the lawn mower. Bo felt around inside, shifting grimy rags and clumps of damp newspaper before turning to Harvey. "Damn Dominican girl sold me the car with no spare."

"You ain't check when you bought it?"

"She was foin, foin, foin."

"You got Triple A?"

"Yes. No. You?"

Harvey didn't even own a car anymore. Bo had a Sears charge card, so they began walking north and to the east, toward Aventura Mall on North Miami Beach, where there was a Sears with an automotive department. There was also a reception going on in the Portrait Studio.

Before Harvey knew it, he was running. Bo's idea: "Let's race the rest of the way."

He had cleared his head by smoking the remainder of Bo's joint, and he was so angry with everything, it was like he could scarcely feel his hip. He slapped his foot down hard, and there was only a dull acknowledgment. Coach Red should see me now, he thought. Now I'm focused.

He ran at a jogger's pace and in five minutes had overtaken Bo, who had shot off at full stride. Bo was panting and holding his stomach as Harvey pulled even, then passed him. Harvey ran this way every day as a part of his conditioning regimen. Bo, on the other hand, drank too much, smoked too much weed, and was good at making excuses to avoid the weight room. Bo is perfect for the Kumquat League, Harvey thought, but they cut *me* from the team.

"Lemme rest, then we start over," Bo gasped.

"Naw," said Harvey. He could have widened the gap between them if he wanted. He closed his eyes. It was just like back in college when he had worn the cleats the sports agent gave him. They glowed in the dark. You couldn't touch Harvey Benjamin once he caught the ball, man, not in those shoes. Most touchdowns in a game. Most touchdowns in a season, longest reception in Peach Bowl history—99 yards as a junior. They hit him so hard, he was puking on the sidelines. Felt like his bones were held together by rubber bands, his skull a container of broken glass. But he kept going back out, like a warrior. Took that ball 99 yards. He was destined for great things. Wait til next year!

But against Baylor, they broke his hip. He spent senior year in a cast. Then came love, pregnancies, old teammates kickin' it large in the big ranks who forgot his name, geeks like Roderick moving in on his woman. Rent. And the subsequent investigation made him give the shoes back. They were all connected, these betrayals.

"Ain't no crybabies in football," Harvey said, as he opened his eyes in flat, green North Miami Beach. Glancing down at his cheap shoes slapping against the asphalt, he thought, my limp ain't that obvious.

Then he heard Bo say: "Y'all got us. That's fo'sho'real."

Without breaking his stride, he looked over his shoulder to see Bo bent over the trunk of a police car. The white officer held a gun on Bo while the black officer, who had cheeks that sagged like a bulldog's, patted his buttocks and thighs for weapons.

The officer in the police car approaching Harvey squawked through a megaphone: "Halt. Get down on the ground."

Harvey knew the police were making a mistake in arresting him and Bo; just as he and Bo had made a mistake in running through this quiet neighborhood. The police would detain them for a few minutes and then realize that they were inno-

cent of any criminal activities. Harvey would mention the flat tire if Bo didn't blurt
it out first. If these were nice cops, they might even give him and Bo a lift to the
mall.

Instead of stopping, however, Harvey picked up speed.

The chase proceeded east on the usually quiet Northeast 186th Street. The
second police car was right on Harvey's tail, but a car has no hands and cannot
grab. The officer driving the police car boomed: "Get down on the ground now!"
The car was only about five yards behind him. If the officer wanted to, he could
have rammed him, but now the siren had brought people out of their houses. Harvey knew in front of such an audience, they wouldn't ram him unless they had to.

A little girl waved from the yard of the Goldsmith home. He had cut their
lawn twice last month. Too many prickly spurs, so he had worn long pants. Mr.
Goldsmith had paid with a check and asked him to fill out a tax form. Harvey
waved back, but Ruth, Mrs. Goldsmith, pulled her daughter inside.

When the female officer lunged from the patrol car, Harvey, who had been
inhaling through his nose and exhaling through his mouth to save his strength,
surged out of reach. The female officer, a tall, sexy señorita from what Harvey could
see, did not give up the chase, though her cap had fallen off and now she lagged
behind even the patrol car. Cursing, she ran with a black baton raised in her hand.
When she caught Harvey, innocent or guilty, it was clear by her grunts that she was
going to club him hard. She was tough, probably played ball in her day, but in
women's games, the rules are easier.

"This ain't slow pitch, bitch," Harvey said, between breaths.

The tall woman with the baton lost ground.

The first police car joined the second. The two vehicles together blocked both
sides of the street, so you couldn't go east or west on Northeast 186th. Bo Deckle's
voice squawked from the first police car: "Why you running, Harvey? They just
want to ask us some questions, and we ain't done nothin' but smoke a little joint."

What an ignorant thing to say, Harvey thought, as he moved from the middle
of the street and began to run along the sidewalk. His instincts told him now that
the first police car, the one with "Sergeant" painted on the hood, intended to ram
him. The siren wailed. And there was that other sound, too, a horn that reported
like a loud goose. The sergeant car knocked over two trash cans and a red-barn
mailbox and flattened a plastic duck and her ducklings. If the sergeant car rammed
him, it would reinjure his hip, so Harvey ran closer to the houses, but not too close.
Some civilian hero might lose his head and tackle him from the sidelines. That fat
man in the housecoat chomping a cigar, for example. Or those teenagers in the
backwards baseball caps. Everybody wants to jump you when you're down.

The amplified voices insisted: "Stop. Stop," and Harvey Benjamin began to feel his hip again.

"You got to play through pain." He was coming down, the pain increasing. He realized he was in a lot of trouble . . . if he stopped.

This was a mistake.

But if Priscilla hadn't-a disrespected him, then he maybe wouldn't be running in the first damned place. Here he was doing all he could to keep the family together, cutting grass, playing Kumquat ball, and she goes and forgets her birth control pills after he had told her again and again they couldn't afford no more children until he made it to the pros.

Then Priscilla, suffering with dizzy spells, lost so many days from the Portrait Studio that nothing was left in the savings account. They were about to lose the apartment. How did she expect him to feed everybody and pay rent too? He had wanted to buy a car, a pair of shoes like back in college, maybe a playpen for when the kid was born. And here was Priscilla getting sick every other day and ignoring him when he talked sense.

"No welfare," she said in the taxi on the way back from another trip to the hospital, and she was the one who had screwed up and gotten pregnant again.

"Then I just don't know," Harvey said. "What you expect is gon' happen to us?"

"Roderick can get you a job at the Portrait Studio."

"What do I know about picture taking?"

"You'll have benefits."

"I'm an athlete."

"An athlete trying to put his girlfriend on welfare."

"Who be puttin' this kind-a childish shit in your head?"

The cabby, a Haitian man who exposed his gums when he smiled, turned in his seat to pass Harvey a look. Harvey nodded at him: Women.

He said to Priscilla, "It's just for a little while so we don't lose the apartment. Stop actin' so young minded."

"Age has nothing to do with it. My mother and father struggled their whole life to make something of themselves, and me. As long as we're healthy, we shouldn't take handouts."

"You ain't healthy." Harvey pursed his lips. "Ain't no shame in welfare. People do what they gotta to do."

Priscilla made an indignant sound. "Well, do what you gotta do, but I'm not going on welfare like some of your other little freaks."

"Freaks?"

"Hoes. Whores. Whatever."

Harvey thought, there she goes with that shit again, as the cabby pulled into a parking space. Harvey got out and opened Priscilla's door, but he didn't offer his hand. He didn't want to touch her. Who she think she is callin' somebody a whore? He passed the cabby two tens, accepted the change from the man but did not offer a tip. Yes, there were other women before and yes he had other children, but whores? "Whores?" Harvey said.

"Whores. Hoes. Whores."

"Now you being funny. Now you making fun of people."

"Call them what you want, I ain't one of them." Walking was a chore for Priscilla, but Harvey didn't offer an arm. She was a big, fat, black waddling duck, is all. "I'm not going to let you drag me down to their level."

"You talkin' about my momma?"

"I ain't talking about your momma."

"Matter-a fact, I shoulda done what my momma told me to do. Maybe I'm too dumb to understand it," said Harvey shaking his head, failing to notice that some-one had pissed on the stairs. He stepped in the rancid puddle and cursed. "But you should be the last one to talk. Look in the mirror. If whores was such a bad thing, I shoulda dumped you a long, long time ago. That's what my momma told me to do." It was the meanest line he had ever wanted to say to her, but still he turned and added: "Bitch."

"Who you calling bitch?"

"Who was that boy who stuck them fingers in your pants?"

"Liar!" In spite of her condition, she caught up with him on the stairs and grabbed his arm. "Nothing happened. You are my first, my only. And you know it."

"I don't know nothin'."

As they reached their landing, he whipped his arm out of her grasp. She sighed and dug into her purse for the keys.

"You confessed. You admitted it. The only part you left out was that you actual-ly let him go all the way, like I'm so stupid. You think I'm so stupid. I don't know nothin'."

"You are my only, Harvey."

"Bullshit."

"You're bullshit with your broke ass."

"Well, well, I see now," he said, as though this were the real source of his anger. "You kissed him back. You admitted it. You led him on, with your big goofy self. You was already pregnant with my babies, but you kissed him back. I was a fool for letting you go to that shitty prom. But I was trying to be nice to you, didn't want to spoil your little childhood. That's why a man shouldn't be nice to no bitch. F'all I know, you probably sucked his dick."

"This is so stupid. This is so stupid. I told you this like a hundred times. But that's how you wanna act, shouting my business to the whole building." She man-aged to insert her key and open the door. "You could at least act civilized, Harvey. Get your ass out of the jungle."

Priscilla nodded to the apartment across the hall, where the neighbor was keeping the twins until she and Harvey had returned from Jackson Memorial where the doctor had assured them that the baby who would soon be dead was fine. Harvey was not about to go get the twins. First, they had to decide what she meant by that last comment.

"Jungle? Jungle?" he said hopping. "You blacker than me!" He would have added "And I have better hair," but she brushed it aside.

"I knew you would go there. That's not even what I'm talking about. I should never have told you my private business. You can't understand anything except how to be mean."

"Mean? I'm good. Shit. I done you a favor." Harvey walked into the apartment behind her, slamming the door. His hip was on fire. "I could-a left your ass when I found out. But I stayed. All those girls I had, but I stayed with your black ass."

"Stop calling me that!"

"You don't like it, but you can call me dummy and stupid."

"Stop calling me that." She was crying now.

"Shoe black."

"Leave the house, Harvey. Please leave," she said. When she turned on him, she was not crying anymore, and he saw what this was all about. Priscilla had given up a basketball scholarship to the University of Central Florida for the twins, for him. She would have made a great attorney. Everyone said so. He was just a dumb jock, and a failure at that. Oh, if he had made money, she'd-a been happy on the gravy train. But now her black ass was too proud to be with him. Priscilla set her purse on one of the boxes of clothes, dishes, and toys that had been packed and stacked against the wall anticipating eviction. Everybody wants to jump you when you're down. Priscilla was just like the rest of them. "Leave," she said, "Leave," mocking him with her sudden calm, her proper talking, "but do keep your voice down. Unless this conversation is of concern to me, you, and the neighbors as well."

The "as well" sent him over the brink. "You lucky I'm a good man," he shouted. "After what you done, some men woulda beat the hell out of you."

Priscilla stretched to her full height, as tall as him. "If you so much as lay a hand on me, Harvey Benjamin, I will beat the hell out of *you*."

It was ridiculous, really. She was just throwing his own words back at him. How could she possibly beat the hell out of him at five months pregnant? He was a man, and well conditioned, never mind that she was tall for a woman. In fact, she was his woman, his baby momma. She had no right to stand there with her hands on her hips, her shoulders thrown back, acting like she was doing him a favor. He was the man.

Harvey slapped Priscilla.

"Beat who?" he said, slapping her shocked mouth a second and third time. He put her in a headlock when she tried to claw his eyes. "Beat me?" He pushed her to the ground. She fell against a box of towels and sheets, crushing it. He began to kick her.

"O my good God!"

"Beat me?"

"You're killing me!"

"Beat me? Beat me?" Harvey was crying now too, and gagging on the odor of bleach. He was only just sane enough to pull back when he realized he was kicking her in the stomach.

The police were getting smart. The female officer had set herself up in a crouch on the hood of the second police car, the baton raised high above her head. She was ready to leap. The second police car had shot on up ahead and then done an about-face to cut off Harvey's escape.

Harvey turned off into a large unfenced yard on the left side of the street. In the back yard he skirted a swimming pool drained of water. In the bottom of the dry pool, a pimply man and woman, naked except for their sunglasses, lay stretched out on folding chairs. Their collie rose up on its hind legs and barked. Now he was headed north. Aventura Mall would be just across the railroad tracks, which he was certain ran just behind the next house, a magnificent pastel green one with badly sculpted hedges. The police car with the woman on the hood drove up on the grass behind Harvey and stopped just short of killing the collie. Tires spun in the lovely flower bed, flinging white roses and peach hibiscus against the trunk of a ficus tree and onto the heads of the suddenly roused sunbathers looking up and out from over the edge of their pool.

The female officer jumped off the hood, but already she was huffing and puffing.

"You need conditioning, *chica*," Harvey said, exhaling through his mouth, blood flowing from his nostrils. That's what's wrong with women, he thought. Men play hard and long because they're conditioned. Men take the game serious.

Harvey sniffed the blood back into his nose, sucked it into his mouth, and realized that it was his own blood that smelled so terribly like bleach.

Bo Deckle squawked: "Don't know where you going, Harvey, but you goin', that's fo'sho'real."

Harvey reached the tracks, slipping and stumbling until he got his footing on the mound of gravel they ran on. He followed the iron rails as angry voices trailed behind him. Out of the corner of his eye, he saw that now other police officers had joined the chase, batons raised. They had brought their dogs, too. This was a mistake, a mistake that could only end one way, and Harvey would take it like a man—even if he shielded his hip.

Looking up, he saw Biscayne Boulevard, and beyond that, Aventura Mall, dominating the skyline like a concrete mountain. He turned east again, crossing the tracks, then passing into the middle of Biscayne Boulevard, one of Miami's busiest roadways during rush hour. He ignored the traffic, which halted with a terrible screeching of tires before him. There was the sound of an angry collision, and he thought of the dead baby, but he did not turn to see what had hit what. If he stopped, that would be all his fault, too.

"But if I keep running, it ain't my fault."

He ran across the parking lot with a final burst. People with bags ducked out of his way. He reached the glass doors of the mall, the entrance to Sears. He opened the doors, pushed his way inside. Someone grabbed him from behind, but Harvey thought, hold on if you want! Mustering what strength was left in his legs, he dragged this burden—the sexy señorita, the slow pitch softball queen, Miss Women's Basketball League, spitting and clawing—the remaining ten yards past the neatly folded pillowcases of domestics right to the open door of the Portrait Studio.

Priscilla wore a blue, form-fitting dress with a frilly collar, and there was Roderick putting cake in her mouth. With her hair piled up high off her forehead, she was as beautiful as she'd ever been, even if her ears stood out. The backdrop was Hawaii, and everyone had cameras, plastic leis, blue jeans. The twins he spotted dancing together near the punch bowl.

As Harvey bulled over the threshold and lunged at the surprised newlyweds, the police fell upon him with a great fury.

The twins screamed, and Priscilla shouted, "O my good God, Harvey!"

The police rained down blows, and Harvey could feel them shattering bone, but much too late. He punched Roderick's stupid, lightweight ass to the floor and got his arms around Priscilla.

"I ain't gon' hit you, baby," he said. "I love you. I love you."

His head against her breasts slid slowly down to her waist from all the pulling and pummeling. He grimaced from the pain of the hip knocked from its socket by the angry police officers, but he would not let go of Priscilla. She was smart, she was beautiful, she was his woman, with her hair piled up high, oh and when she smiled, she was more than beautiful. She clawed at his eyes. Her nails pierced his cheeks.

He was trying to explain, but she—

And the blows. He thought he heard someone say, "The game is over," but it might just as easily have been something else. He felt another bone shatter, he was losing consciousness, but Harvey the warrior would not let go. He had to let her know that they were united together forever. His fingers interlocked, he clung to the best catch of his career and said, "Nobody gon' marry my baby momma but me. Will you marry me, Priscilla, please?"

She kept digging into his cheeks. He felt her nails biting his cheeks. He tried to wait for her answer as the police rained down blows. But he lost consciousness.

Apostate

In two weeks I would be leaving Miami for Gainesville to enroll as a freshman at the University of Florida. I was eighteen and eager to get away from the widow and end our shameful affair. I would go away and, with God's help, come back a new man and a better Christian.

My father wanted me to study engineering because he had heard there was good money in it—even though engineers didn't get a chance to actually drive the train. My mother, disappointed that I had chosen not to go into the ministry, wanted me to work towards a degree in social work, which she felt was the next best way to use my education in the service of the Lord. My grandmother, too, was saddened when I turned down my scholarship to Bible College.

"Be a teacher, Elwyn," my grandmother suggested. "Then when you come back, you can be superintendent of the Sunday School program. Many of our Sunday chool teachers just don't know how to reach our kids. We're losing them to the streets."

"I don't want to teach," I protested. Teachers were not my favorite people.

Just a few months earlier, I had attended the senior awards program at my high school and suffered my greatest humiliation. The principal, Mr. Byrd, in announcing the winners of the Grand Gopher Awards, deliberately stuttered: "El-El—"

I rose to my feet thinking he was about to say my name, "Elwyn Parker," which was not a haughty presumption, for he was nearing the "P's" and I had been, at least during my junior and senior years, an outstanding gopher. Over the final two years, no one had achieved a higher grade point average with as rigorous a course load as I carried—all advanced placement classes, all A's. No one had been better known around campus than I, by students and faculty alike, and no one more feared. For I had been exact and courageous in doing all that my Lord had commanded. My confrontations with the secular school administration had become famous. I had been interviewed by the local newspaper too many times to count, so even the surrounding community had been aware of me.

Finally, no one had presided over a school club with as many members, or as much influence, as the one I had founded and headed, the Jesus Club. At our largest, we numbered 150; it was through our efforts that the administration was forced to change the school's nickname, which had been around since the school opened thirty years before, from Red Devils to Gophers.

Thus, I stood when Mr. Byrd said "El-El" because I deserved a Grand Gopher, deserved to have my senior picture hang permanently in the Gopher Hall of Fame.

"El-El-Eldridge Pomerantz," Mr. Byrd said.

I sat down quickly, but the damage was done. All around me, people were chuckling.

As Eldridge Pomerantz, a second-string football player who had been a regular at our prayer meetings until he made first string, took his place on the stage next to the other Grand Gophers, Mr. Byrd's eyes met mine, and I recall that he smiled. Another battle won by Satan.

But he was wrong. While the administration did not bestow upon me one single popularity prize that gloomy awards night, I did march to the stage four times to collect awards that had stipends attached to them: National Merit Award, $2000; The Young Musicians Award, $800; The National Christian Scholarship, $500; and from the Jesus Club, the Blessed Gopher Award, of which I was the first recipient, $298.

In truth, I didn't know what I wanted to study in college—music, medicine, and anthropology all interested me—but if Mr. Byrd were an example of what a teacher is— petty, mean, vengeful—then no, I didn't want to be a teacher.

There was one more thing I didn't want to be, an attorney. Sister Morrisohn's late husband, Buford, had been an attorney, so she pushed for me to study law.

"Then when we marry," she explained, "it'll be like it used to be."

Sister Morrisohn had to be kidding, of course. I was eighteen. She was forty-five. Marriage was ludicrous. But as the time of my departure for college grew nearer, she had been kidding in that manner much too frequently to suit me. Her strange taste in humor gave me headaches.

Was it but a week ago that we visited the mall where she bought my going-away gift, the expensive leather briefcase with dual combination locks and hidden compartment for toothbrush and floss?

As always, Sister Morrisohn and I behaved in public as mother and son. While "mother" paid for the briefcase, "son" witnessed to a sixteen-year-old girl who had wandered into the store.

Yes, the girl attended church. A Methodist.

Yes, she knew about Jesus. Who didn't?

No, she hadn't accepted Him as personal savior, but she would when she was older, she said. Too much living to do now.

Take a look at this, I said to the girl, and I made to reach into my jacket pocket for a tract ("We Know Not the Hour When Death Shall Appear") but found my hand detained by Sister Morrisohn.

She kissed me on the mouth. "Let's go, hubby."

I jerked my hand out of her grasp but followed her out of the store, forgetting to give the confused sixteen-year-old the tract which might have led to her salvation.

I was so shaken, I didn't say a word until we reached her house.

"Why would you do a thing like that?"

"I was just kidding," she said.

"Someone from the church could've been passing by."

"No one saw. I checked first."

"It's dangerous. Crazy."

"You liked it though, didn't you?"

"No. It made me very nervous."

"You liked that girl, didn't you?" she said.

"I was just doing the Lord's work."

She grew silent. My devotion to the Lord always seemed to surprise her. It was true I had sinned—and would perhaps continue sinning until I put some distance between us—but I was not the great hypocrite Sister Morrisohn was. I had not hardened my heart against God.

While I prayed every night for forgiveness, she had gradually, if however discreetly, become a backslider. Once again she took pleasure in the things of the world—cigarettes, which she admitted she had never truly given up; wine, which she insisted helped her forget that she was a poor widow spending all too much time with a lover a third her age; and those melancholy Jim Reeves records. Not his hymns, mind you! But those monotonous, two-step odes to heartbreak and unrequited love. How I grew to dread that brooding baritone. She often played her favorite, "Distant Drums," as a prelude to our sordid communion:

> *I hear the sound, of distant drums*
> *Far away, far away*
> *And if they call for me to come*
> *Then I must go, and you must stay*

She asked me to teach her how to play "Distant Drums" on the piano, but I refused. At least she could not get me to do that.

So there we were after she had kissed me in the mall.

"I'm not interested in the girl. I was just doing the Lord's work," I said to her.

Sister Morrisohn seemed on the verge of either laughter or tears. "Do you love me, Elwyn?" she said.

"Let's not get into this—"

"I'm nothing to you," she said. "You're just using me. All I am is your harlot."

"Don't say that."

"I'm a fallen woman. You could never love me."

"That's not true."

"I wish Buford were here. You don't love me."

"That's not true."

"Then say it," she said. "Say it, Elwyn."

She had that kind of power over me. She must have known I did not love her. She certainly knew I could not risk losing her. I cried, "I love you! I love you!"

She smiled. "I don't believe you." We were alone in her house. She moved close to me. She loosened her clothes. I should have turned my head. I should have prayed for God to deliver me. But no matter how many times I drank from the fountain, I found myself yet thirsting. "Touch me when you say you love me," she said.

I touched her. I became aroused—this for a woman who had posed as my mother but a few hours before. "I love you."

We were on the bed. Our clothes were piled on top of the new leather briefcase on the floor. "Say it with feeling," she said.

As we moved, I felt many things, and I used some of these things to say it the way she wanted me to say it. "I love you."

It was, of course, a complete lie, but Sister Morrisohn didn't seem to notice. She hummed, but no matter—I still heard the words.

Then I must go, and you must stay

The wages of sin, it turns out, is not always death: sometimes it's a life of Jim Reeves records.

My grandmother said, "So what's wrong with being a teacher?" She spoke to my back; I watched her in the mirror. She had gotten so large that she had to use her hands to lift her legs, one at a time, up onto my bed, where at last she stretched out, exhausted. She fanned herself with a hand, breathed through her mouth. "He made some preachers; He made some teachers."

I said, "I just don't think He's calling me to teach, Gran'ma."

"Well, your students say you're a better piano teacher than Sister McGowan, and nobody, not even Pastor, can explain scripture like you."

"Well, Gran'ma, I don't know." My mother handed me a black tie. I slipped it around my collar and began the first loop of a double Windsor. I liked a thick knot.

"No. Wear your good white shirt," my mother fussed. "This one makes the tie fit funny." She turned and began searching the closet for my good white shirt.

"I like this shirt, Mom." But already I was beginning to unfasten the tie.

"Turn around," my father said. There he was with his new camera. "I want to take a picture."

I turned. "But I'm not wearing any pants," I said.

"So? Now hold the tie like you're fixing it. No, don't smile. Act natural," he said. The camera flashed. "It's a work of art. Young Man Dressing."

"He's not going to wear that tie either," my mother said. She just couldn't make up her mind. Now she held the new blue one in her hand. "The church valedictorian's got to look his best."

I took the good white shirt and the new blue tie from my mother.

My father snapped a shot before I could put them on—just me in my Fruit of the Looms. "This one's even better. I'm going to put this one in the church yearbook."

"No you won't," said my grandmother. As she lay, propped up on her side, she might have been a Peter Paul Rubens woman—in print dress, and with ankles swollen by diabetes. "People won't know what to make of this family." She trembled with laughter, two fingers covering her mouth.

My father grinned. "He's not just smart and talented and a great warrior for the Lord, he's the flower of manhood." My father posed in accordance with the Marquis of Queensberry and when I blocked right, he landed one with a left. It hurt only just a little. "Feel that. Solid!"

"Stop it. Stop it." My grandmother, slapping her thighs now, laughed until she coughed. "You two. Oh, what a blessing."

I put on my shirt, buttoned it, slipped the new tie around my collar.

"Take a picture," said my father. He handed the camera to my mother. He put an arm around my shoulder. One more inch and I'd be as tall as he was.

"Let me at least put on my pants," I said.

My father laughed. "No." He wasn't holding me so firmly that I couldn't break away. We were having a good time.

"Take off your hat," said my mother behind the camera.

My father protested. "The bald spot."

"They already know," said my grandmother and mother in unison.

We all laughed at that, even my father doffing his school bus driver's cap. It amused us when we said the same thing at the same time. We were a family.

"Snap the picture," my father said.

"Something's wrong," my mother said. "Your collar's too large. That's not your good shirt."

I looked down at my shirt. She was right. It was Brother Morrisohn's good shirt.

"Where did you get that?" my mother said.

"Sister Morrisohn gave it to me," I said in an offhand way, like don't you remember when she gave it to me, Mom? You were there. You were definitely there, so don't ask any more questions. I only have two more weeks in Miami, and when I return, I promise I'll be your son again. "A gift," I said.

My father tested the sleeve with thumb and forefinger. "That's very nice of her. This is good material."

"Rich. But why would she give you a white shirt?" said my mother. "Pink, green, blue I could understand."

"I don't know," I said. "She's old fashioned."

"Graduation gift?" suggested my grandmother.

"No," said my mother, "I've seen this shirt in the laundry more than a few times and meant to ask you about it. When did she give it to you?"

"I'm not sure," I said. I had to remain calm, nonchalant. I had to derail her instinctive suspicion. "I think she gave it to me after I taught her to play "In Love Abiding Jesus Came." That was Brother Morrisohn's favorite hymn. It's a dopey gift."

"Don't call a gift dopey, Elwyn," warned my grandmother. "All gifts come from God."

"Sorry, Gran'ma."

"Bridle your tongue, Elwyn. Buford, rest his soul, and Elaine Morrisohn are very dear friends of mine. They have always been fond of you." My grandmother pulled herself to a sitting position. "Buford, if you recall, bought that piano for you. You didn't think the piano was such a dopey gift, did you?"

"No, Gran'ma."

"Elaine was your first piano student. It's not so dopey when she puts ten dollars in your hand for a half-hour's work, is it?"

"No, Gran'ma."

"With all the blessings God has given you, I should think you'd be the last to bite the hand that feeds you. Here you are on the eve of manhood, getting dressed to go to church and pick up a scholarship funded by the same woman who gave you a dopey gift."

The Buford Morrisohn Scholarship for the Outstanding College-Bound Christian, $4000, of which I was the first recipient.

"Sorry, Gran'ma."

"Don't let me hear such rubbish again." My grandmother signaled for her four-pronged walker. I passed it to her. My father and I helped her to her feet. "I love you, Elwyn, but you'd better pray that God never takes back any of your dopey gifts."

My grandmother lumbered out of the room. My mother and father, shaking their heads, soon followed. I finished dressing alone.

It had worked.

My mother had left without asking the one question I could little answer: By the way, Elwyn, where is your good white shirt?

I certainly could not tell her that on that night more than a year ago when Sister Morrisohn had finally mastered the chord changes of "In Love Abiding Jesus Came," there had been a dinner set on the floor in the fashion of the Chinese with all the romantic trappings, and afterwards someone's happy foot knocked over a candle and destroyed the sleeve of a good white shirt, which by all means had to be replaced.

I couldn't just walk into our house with a charred sleeve.

Oh, that? As the widow Morrisohn and I were making love . . . .

And I certainly couldn't have entered our home barebacked.

Yes, Dad, it is a solid chest, isn't it? Quite manly! Those aren't birth marks. Tonight during climax the widow used her teeth.

So instead, I had accepted Sister Morrisohn's gift of one of Brother Morrisohn's shirts.

"They look the same," she had said. "I never noticed it before, but you're about his size."

And that's when she started with the Elwyn-marry-me jokes.

Not even John on the Isle of Patmos had such hellish visions of the future.

Two o'clock in the afternoon on a Saturday in August, the Church of Our Blessed Redeemer Who Walked Upon the Waters was packed for the awards ceremony.

I got up from the piano when they told me to get up, and I marched across the pulpit.

I stood where they wanted me to stand, at the head of a line of about thirty recently graduated high-schoolers. I could neither see the pews nor the floor, just three hundred brown faces floating above a sea of sharp suits and pretty dresses. Body heat negated the effects of the air conditioner. Sweat poured down my brow.

In my valedictory address, I said what they wanted me to say: The future is for the children of God. Satan's days are numbered, for with Christ in our vessel, we can smile at the storm—and so on, and so on, to thunderous applause.

Then I collected my Buford Morrisohn Scholarship for the Outstanding College-Bound Christian and sat back at the piano to close the service.

When it was all over, I mingled with my fellows and our parents (and grandparents), congratulating those who had received lesser scholarships, and receiving congratulations for my own award.

Then the larger crowd descended upon us. From every mouth there came the same questions:

"Where are you going to college?"

(As though you don't already know.)

"When are you leaving?"

(Not soon enough.)

"Are you excited?"

(Relieved.)

Everyone seemed to want to shake my hand, and I politely acquiesced, though I was eager to get away from the church grounds. I hoped to avoid Sister Morrisohn, who had been giving me the eye all through service.

Besides, my parents were throwing an after-party for me at home where I could celebrate in safety.

Outside, small children dressed in their best clothes played with reckless energy, running and hitting and screaming and falling and getting up again. I ducked out of the way of a running one pursued by an angry one waving a hymnal over his head like the two tablets of stone. Another one said a naughty word, and I chastised her.

"It slipped out," she said.

Where were our children picking up such terrible language? I scolded, "You want to grow up good so Jesus can take you to Heaven, OK?"

The child was absolutely precious. Pigtails and ribbons and black patent-leather shoes. "When will I go to heaven?"

"When you die," I said.

"Oh," said the girl, whom I recognized as Brother and Sister Naylor's youngest. "So can I go play now?"

"Yes," I said.

"Thank-you-Jesus," she said, and she skipped away.

I walked to my old Mazda. I opened the door, slipped inside, slammed the door, started the car. Sister Morrisohn, appearing out of nowhere, knocked on my windshield.

"Hey," she said.

I rolled down the window. Up close, under her perfume, I smelled alcohol. She had been drinking wine again. She wore a blue church dress with a modest collar, but when she leaned against the car, almost passing her head through the window, the modest collar hung loose around her neck revealing that she was wearing no brassiere.

She had never behaved this way on church grounds before.

I pulled away when she made a sudden move, thinking she was trying to kiss me as she had in the mall.

"Hey," she said, passing me a greeting card. "Congratulations on your graduation."

"Thanks."

Raising her head, she checked to see that no one was near enough to hear. "We haven't been together in a week. Why are you avoiding me?"

"We'll talk later."

"Was it the mall?" she whispered.

"Yes. The mall."

She made a silly face. "That was a joke. No one saw. I swear."

"It's too risky. And it's so wrong. We're Christians," I said. "We're the light of the world."

She sighed. "You don't plan to see me anymore."

"I don't," I said.

"This is the end."

"Yes."

"When you said you loved me, did you mean it, Christian?"

"Could we talk later?" I said.

Her eyes blinked nervously. "Tell me now. Did you mean it?"

"No," I said.

She nodded her head. "Yes you did. Yes you did."

"Sister Morrisohn," I said. "We have to get on with our lives. We have to wake up. What we did can lead to nowhere good."

She said, "Look, Elwyn, we're not going to get married. That's impossible. You're just a kid. I'm . . . mature. Too bad. But you can't tell me you don't love me because no matter where you go or what you do, I'll always love you." She put her hands together as in prayer. "And I know you love me."

"I'm sorry," I said.

"You're not sorry. You're scared. What we did may seem wicked in the eyes of the church, but it is real. You know it's real."

"I want to go to heaven when I die."

"So that makes it OK to step on my feelings? To use me?"

"I didn't use you," I said.

"Then you loved me?"

I didn't answer. I wasn't sure anymore that I knew the answer. Why did I feel it necessary to go to another city? Why hadn't I broken it off before?

"Love is never a sin," she said.

"Bye," I said.

"Come by tonight. Let me prove your love."

"Sister Morri—"

"Just one last time, then it's over forever," she said. "Go on with your life, pretend you don't love me."

"No." Help me, Lord. "No, I won't."

"Just one last time." She smoothed the hairs on my arm. "Then I'll let you go."

"OK," I said. Already I had become aroused. "One last time."

"You won't be sorry."

"OK," I said. I put the Mazda in reverse. "Bye."

"See you later," Sister Morrisohn said. And then: "You look very good in his shirt."

The party that took place afterwards was a lot like the awards ceremony, except that there weren't so many people—just my parents, my grandmother, my best friends from church, and several members of the Jesus Club from school. The Rev. James Cleveland boomed "Lord, Do It" from the record player. There was turkey and ham and collard greens on the table. Hugs, congratulations, and the unavoidable questions abounded: "So where are you going to college?", "Excited, aren't you?", "Can we get together before you leave?".

My mother said, "It's your party, Elwyn. You say Grace."

"Lord, bless this food that it may give us the strength to do your will."

"Amen," we all said.

My father said, "Dig in."

We ate, we laughed, we cried. After I straighten out my problems with Sister Morrisohn, I thought, I shall be able to take genuine pleasure from such fellowship divine. As it was, I was eager for the party to be over. The Devil yet had full control of my hormones.

I was not the only one eager for the party to end. Eldridge Pomerantz, the Grand Gopher himself, was there. He had avoided me all afternoon, still fearing the power of God.

Now he sat at my piano with Sabina, the less bubbly half of the Anderson twins. Sabina played the right hand of "The Old Rugged Cross," Eldridge the left. She had already begun taking classes at Miami-Dade Junior College, where she was a powerful witness for the Lord. He was leaving in two weeks for Pennsylvania to play football and study architecture at the University of Pittsburgh.

I approached them.

"Elwyn," they said.

"Eldridge. Sabina," I said. "I see you're making lovely music together."

"I'm teaching him," Sabina said. "Praise the Lord."

"Praise the Lord," I said.

Eldridge smiled. He was a nice guy, though a backslider. He wouldn't have come to my party had Sabina not been there. They had been in love for about a year.

Accidentally, Eldridge hit an augmented chord. "Oops," he said. "What was that?"

"Sounds good. Play it again," I commanded.

They played the chorus again, using the augmented chord instead of the plain F chord.

"Wow," said Sabina. "We sound like experts."

"The augmented adds another dimension to the song," I said.

And Sabina caught my cue. "Just as Christ adds another dimension to our lives," she said.

Eldridge's spine lost an inch.

"We miss you at Bible study," I said, setting my hand on his wide shoulder.

Eldridge mumbled, "Football practice, you know?"

"I've been telling him," Sabina said, "that football won't get him into Heaven."

"Neither will being a nice guy," I said. "And you're one of the nicest people I know."

"Neither will being married to a Christian," Sabina said. "You've got to seek the Lord for yourself."

"Neither will having your picture hang in your school's hall of fame," I said. "It is only through the Grace of God that ye shall enter the Kingdom of Heaven."

"Mama can't save you."

"Daddy can't save you."

"You've got to seek the Lord for yourself."

"Well," said Eldridge Pomerantz, a boy with thighs like fire hydrants, "I should know better. I'm just waiting—"

"Waiting? Jesus didn't wait to die for your sins!"

Eldridge's eyes darted from me to Sabina to the crowd that had begun to gather. I moved away and watched as the Christians, led by my grandmother—that great old-time saint—descended upon the only unsaved person in the room:

"Seek ye first the Kingdom of God."

"Serve the Lord while ye are yet young."

"Tomorrow's day may never dawn."

"Do you want to lift up your eyes in Hell?"

"Jesus died for you."

The Christians devoured the lion.

After a while, Eldridge fell to his knees and cried out, "Help me. Help me, Jesus."

When the party ended, there were shouts of jubilation. A lost sheep had returned to the fold. No one was more delighted by Eldridge's conversion than I was.

"You must write to me when you get to Pennsylvania," I said.

"Yes, Elwyn," he said, brushing back tears.

"Are you happy?" I said.

"Yes." We moved out of the way so that the new offensive lineman for the Lord could shout and jump for joy. "Hallelujah! I'm going to Heaven."

Now Eldridge was a truly Grand Gopher.

I helped my parents clean up, and then I headed for the door, on my way to the final trial.

My mother stopped me. "Where are you going?"

"To visit an old friend."

"You sure?" said my father.

"What?" I said. They never questioned where I went. I was their good Christian son. Did they suspect? Impossible. With Eldridge still on their mind, how could they?

"A friend. Are you sure?" said my mother. She held the platter with the remains of the turkey in it.

"Yes," I said.

My father laughed awkwardly. "Sorry," he said. "It's just that your grandmother thinks—"

My mother interrupted him. "No! I believe Elwyn. Let him go."

"Good," I said, playing it cool. "Save me the leg."

But they knew. Somehow they knew.

"Where were you?"

I walked into her house, turned, scanned the street, then closed the door. "I think they know."

"Don't be ridiculous. No one saw us in the mall," she said.

"Not the mall. I think..." I could not finish my sentence. All I could do was stare at Sister Morrisohn.

"What?" she said, smiling innocently as though she didn't know what had left me temporarily bereft of speech. As though I should not be at all moved by the vision of her before my eyes—the see-through nightgown that stopped above her waist; the brassiere underneath that thrust her breasts forward but did not cover the nipples; the panties below that were but a cross-section of strings running through her private parts; and everything, her rouge, her lipstick, even the rubies in her earrings, red like the fires of hell. "What?"

"Blessed Jesus."

"Before I married Buford, I was a young woman. I loved him, so I surrendered my youth," she said. She pirouetted. "But many say that at forty-five, I am still striking."

"You are," I said, stricken.

"Of course, the church doesn't allow me to dress as I like." She touched her earrings. "So even those closest to me may not notice my appeal."

"I see," I said.

She led me to the bedroom. She sat down on the bed. I sat down on the bed beside her. I stared at her like an idiot. I reminded myself that I had seen it all before—not like this—but we had been together over two years. I should have more control.

"Would you like me to stand up again?" she said.

"Please."

She stood up. She did a silly dance. I drank her in with my eyes. What did it matter? She was mine.

"A relationship should be built on more than physical attraction," she said. She walked over to her stereo. She set the needle on the record. "But when your man goes away, the physical must be foremost on his mind or he will forget."

I hear the sound, of distant drums
Far away, far away

The music did not upset me this time. In fact, I shouted, "Turn it up." She did. Holding her in my arms, I sang along with Jim Reeves and knew that I was no longer a Christian.

And if they call for me to come
Then I must go, and you must stay

"Do you want to have sex with me?" she asked. It was the first time either of us had called it that. "Sex."

"Yes," I said, and we did. And it was good.

Later she said, "Would you like to make love?" It was the first time either of us had called it that. "Making love."

"Yes," I said. "I would like to make love with you, Sister Morrisohn."

"Elaine," she corrected.

"Elaine," I said, and then I made love with her. We made love.

And it was good.

We scrambled for our clothes when we heard the knock at the door.

The knocking did not surprise me as much as it did Elaine. I had been expecting it.

"Sit there at the piano," she told me. She wore her blue church dress and house slippers. She was naked underneath except for the strange brassiere. "We'll say piano lessons, OK?"

I sat at the piano as she commanded, though I knew it was useless. We had taken too long to answer the door. Elaine's face was still rouged.

My grandmother walked in behind her four-pronged walker. "Give me a firm seat," she said to Elaine. "If I sit in your couch, I'll never get up."

When Elaine ran to the kitchen on her errand, my grandmother stared at me but spoke to someone standing behind her outside on the porch: "You go wait in the car. I have to talk to Sister Morrisohn about something in private."

Who was it? Sister McGowan? Sister Jones? At 75, my grandmother no longer drove. I heard the diminishing footfalls of whoever it was had dropped her off, as my grandmother closed the door. Thus, it was by her design that I did not see the unseen person and, especially, that the unseen person did not see me. Her heart was wroth, but she was still protecting me. It gave me hope.

"Elwyn, Elwyn," my grandmother said.

I looked down at the piano keys.

"You were His best, Elwyn. His best."

✠   ✠   ✠

Sister Morrisohn placed the firm-backed chair in the middle of the living room, and my grandmother sat down heavily. She leaned forward, one hand holding the walker for support.

Sister Morrisohn rubbed her hands together nervously. She said, "Can I get you something to drink?"

"Drink!" My grandmother shook her head in disbelief. "There'll be scarce little to drink where you're going."

Sister Morrisohn sank down heavily in the couch, her head bowed.

"I can't believe that a woman of your age would take advantage of a poor, innocent child of God," My grandmother said. "Aren't there enough slack-leg Johnnies with whom you can satisfy your vile, pagan lust? When it burns down there, why don't you just run to the nursery and throw yourself on the infant with the fattest diaper?"

Sister Morrisohn sobbed.

My grandmother said, "Thou thankless apostate, thou creeping Jezebel. The stink of thine iniquity rises to the nostrils of God."

Sister Morrisohn wrapped her arms around herself.

My grandmother said, "You should be flung from the highest tower. And when you burst open, the dogs should pick your rotting flesh from your putrid bones."

Sister Morrisohn cried out, "Oh God, what have I done? What have I done?"

This went on for many minutes, this exhorting, this lamenting. I trembled not only because my turn would come soon, but because Sister Morrisohn's pain was my pain. I wanted to put a hand over my grandmother's mouth.

My grandmother said, "You are lucky that Christ is faithful and able to forgive us our sins. If it were me . . . but Christ the Redeemer died on the cross. Confess your sin, O daughter of Babylon. Confess before this humble servant of God."

And Sister Morrisohn confessed.

And confessed and confessed the entire two-and-a-half years of our affair. Her memory was astonishing. It brought tears to my grandmother's eyes and set her head to nodding from side to side. But for me, each moment that had become part of the dull amalgam in my mind was reclaimed, whole, distinct, animated, golden. I wanted to shout: "Yes, I remember the Fort Lauderdale Holiday Inn on Sunday between services. I remember the sun on your face at the pool, how your beautiful toes stirred water, then splashed, and every drop for me! Happy Birthday. Happy Birthday, each said. And I was happy. I held you too long and only just made it back in time for Youth Hour."

Sister Morrisohn confessed and then collapsed onto the floor.

My grandmother turned to me: "Elwyn, Elwyn, why did you turn your back on God?"

The tears flowed easily, though I didn't feel much like crying. I wanted to hold Sister Morrisohn, Elaine, and tell her that I remembered.

"Elwyn, you were His greatest servant. You can be His servant again. Confess, confess here before me," my grandmother said. "I'll see to it that no one ever finds out about this, but you must confess. Jesus calls you to confess."

"Yes, Gran'ma."

"He is faithful and just to forgive us."

"Yes, Gran'ma."

"Confess, my child. Confess!"

And so I confessed on that evening two weeks before I drove my Mazda up the Florida Turnpike to Gainesville. I confessed to appease my grandmother. I confessed so that Elaine would know I remembered.

There was but one thing I left unsaid. I could have told my grandmother that as I sat confessing, my mind's eye wandered over the fallen body of Sister Elaine Morrisohn, and I planned how in a few weeks when I returned from college to visit, I would arrive one day earlier than I had told everyone else, and I would spend the night right here in this house with the beautiful, forty-five-year-old woman I loved.

Jim Reeves, of course, would be on the stereo.

Jack-Move

For most of the day, Chapman sat backwards in a chair by the door watching the parking lot that the Rug Emporium shared with Kozar's Barber Shop. Fifty-seven cars pulled up, but who comes to a carpet store on a Wednesday night? At 7:15, the phone rang. He thought, Cricket! It was Jared, inviting him to his gig tonight at the Co Co Rico. He was doing the Madonna and the Judy Garland. Jared pronounced the "Garl" in "Garland" like "Girl."

"No," said Chapman.

"I'll give you money," Jared said. "I've got plenty of money."

"Stop calling me." Chapman hung up the phone. At seven-thirty he counted the receipts and rolled down the door. An hour early. He wasn't going to ride the bus in the dark. Not tonight. Mr. Vangaart should pay more if he wants dedication. Everything I do around here, he thought, now I'm a housesitter, too.

He crossed the street and sat down on the bench next to a hugged-up and kissy couple—he big and black, she white and not so big, her hair pulled back so tight her features were elongated. He smiled at the couple, though they didn't acknowledge him. His spirit had taken to them and their brave, public love. Summer didn't seem fruitless anymore. Chapman wished to give these kids something, for whenever someone lightened his load, this is what he did.

It had been that way in the beginning with Cricket, but he had kept giving long after Cricket had stopped. Then Friday night, after the curry chicken and rice had been cleared from the table, the dishes and pots washed, Chapman said, "I know you're sleeping with Oswald." "Now wait a minute," Cricket said. There followed a melodramatic silence in which Chapman searched Cricket's face, all innocent and moon-shaped, but it was so obvious. Oswald, fat as he was, had money. Then Cricket shouted, "You read my letter!"—like you caught me red-handed, so I'm cheap, but now I know you go through my things when I'm not home. Some confession.

So there Chapman was helping Cricket pack in order to show a brave face—"Is this Nestor Torres CD mine or yours? Yours? Take it!"—when what he really wanted to do was scream: "Don't leave me, baby!" Which is exactly what he did after the door slammed.

But now these kids on the bus bench had given him hope. He tugged the boy's sleeve. "Love or money," he said. "If you have a choice, forget the money. Nothing is so precious as—"

"What?" said the big young man, curling his thick bottom lip under his teeth. He grunted menacingly and leaned toward Chapman, his fist clenched. A warning.

Chapman turned away meekly. It was clear that the young man with the white wool cap drawn down to his eyebrows (in this heat!) was a bully. Chapman might be punished for anything the boy found wrong with him, his hairstyle, his clothes, his eyes—all too dangerously vain. He was especially careful to ignore the rude, black-talking white girl with the severe features who spoke, not to him, but at him: "Some people crazy. Some people real crazy."

Chapman simply hated riding the bus. Cricket was the one with the car. Oh Cricket.

He was the last to get on. He paid his fare with a nod to the driver, the same humming woman who had dropped him home yesterday. It was a clean bus, one of the new models with the windows that didn't open except in emergencies. He found a seat toward the back with the sports section of the newspaper in it. He read—what did he read? Nothing. He saw Cricket's pouty face. He put the paper down. The bus rolled through neglected neighborhoods.

In the seat ahead of Chapman's, two boys flipped through a wad of hundred-dollar bills. They wore geometric haircuts and gold earrings. They appeared to be around twelve or thirteen. Maybe they were brothers, or perhaps on an athletic team, wearing identical orange and green sweat suits. The smaller one repeated a line of rap—"Can't touch dis/ Can't touch dis"—as he worked through the stack of money. The larger boy mostly looked out the window but occasionally glowered at anyone he caught staring at his counting friend.

The stack of hundreds was thick, thicker even than in the cash register at the carpet store during Christmas. Chapman said in a voice that was more amazed than loud: "That's a lot of money."

The counter turned. A mouth of gold teeth that spelled something said, "What you say?"

Chapman shook his head quickly. Apologizing. "Nothing, man. It's just so much money."

The big companion leaned over the seat and stabbed Chapman's nose with a bony finger heavy with gold rings. "Slide off, sissy bitch!"

Chapman slid as far back into his seat as he could, put up his hands in a defensive posture. He caught the bus driver's eyes in the rearview mirror, but this wasn't her fight. Chapman told the boys, "I'm sorry."

"Better be." The big boy snorted at his friend in a way that told him he could resume counting. This skinny guy with the funny haircut was no threat. They slapped each other fives. Across the aisle and a few seats up, the big kid from the bus bench whispered something to his girlfriend, who looked back at Chapman, giggling with her chin against her chest.

The smaller boy, the money counter, said to Chapman, "You better push off, man." His upper gold teeth read "2 B-A-D," and the bottom "4 U." He said, "A homeboy try me, I'll step to his ass with a quickness. I'll kick him to sleep."

Chapman was cowed. "I wasn't trying you. But, aren't you scared of getting robbed with all that money?"

The kid with the sentiment on his teeth said, "I got my back. I got my back," and he pointed to the larger boy, nodding agreement beside him. "Right now, we could kick you to sleep and you couldn't do shit about it. Right now."

The bus jerked, and Chapman breathed a sigh of relief. This was his stop.

He did not go directly home, but to the little drinking house near the old men who played dominoes under the trees. He drank two shots of Scotch and left a quarter tip. He watched the domino games with no interest. He decided he'd rent a video. *Dr. Zhivago* or *Silkwood* again. He decided he'd send Cricket a dozen roses by a singing messenger. Maybe Cricket would call him.

When he got to the ATM machine at the bank across the street from his apartment, the sun was all but gone. He knew that he would have to work a second job now that the lease payments were his to make alone. He did his transaction, and the ATM read, "WOULD YOU LIKE ANOTHER TRANSACTION?" and he thought, as though I'm so rich I can make transaction after frigging transaction. Two men appeared out of the semidarkness of the parking lot with stockings over their faces. The short one shoved a gun into Chapman's ribs. The tall, nervous one, who carried no gun, shifted his weight and kept glancing behind himself. There was another one in an old Buick with over-sized whitewalls and a broken window in the back on the driver's side.

Chapman, who had never been robbed before, put his hands up and backed up to the ATM. He recited the Twenty-Third Psalm in his mind: "The Lord is my shepherd . . ."

"This is a jack-move!" the short one growled. "Gimme all your shit!"

Chapman reached into his pockets and pulled everything out. His key ring, the keys to the rug store, his coil of carpet wire, a pen, the wallet with the forty dollars he had just withdrawn from the machine.

The short one grabbed everything from Chapman and passed it to the tall one, who was shaking so much that most of it fell clattering to the ground. "Damn, Homeboy! You dropped it!" said the short one.

The two with the stocking masks knelt to collect what hadn't rolled out of sight.

Chapman continued to recite: "He leadeth me beside the still waters. He restoreth my soul . . ."

"Shut up!" said the short one with the gun trained on Chapman, his other hand scooping up loot.

"He leadeth me in the path of righteousness . . ."

"I told you shut up!" He sprang to his feet, the gun fixed now in his hand like a stone, and pounded the side of Chapman's head.

Thoom!

Chapman collapsed, but reaching out, clutching, and pulled the little one down with him. He didn't weigh as much as a box of throw rugs, writhing and cursing atop Chapman. He struck again.

Thoom!

"Let go."

Thoom!

He struck again, and the gun skated off the side of Chapman's head into darkness. "Homeboy!" he shouted. "Get the gun!"

There was the sound of running feet. Chapman, blinking through the blood pouring from somewhere in his head, continued to hold on. With his arms encircling the other's back, he was stronger than he looked, even with his head bashed in.

"Let go of me! I'm gonna smoke you," the thrasher said.

He held the little body so that it shielded as much of him as possible from the gunfire that he anticipated.

Suddenly, the boy bit Chapman's nose through the hosiery.

Chapman pulled away from the bite, then lunged back and sank his teeth into the boy's cheek.

"Shit. Motherfuck. Homeboy, help me!" The mugger sounded like he was crying. When he raised his head, Chapman saw the hole he had bitten into the boy's stocking mask. His bleeding teeth marks in the boy's cheeks. "Homeboy, help me! Homeboy, where you going?"

Chapman heard tires squealing, as the tall one and the one who had waited in the car sped away.

"Homeboy!" The mugger was heaving and blubbering like a child now. Chapman rolled over and forced him facedown to the pavement. It was easy. He was so small.

"Let go of me! Mother fuck."

He controlled him by folding his arm behind his back like a chicken's wing, then reached out to retrieve the roll of wire from where it had fallen. He bound the mugger with the same regard for symmetry and economy of string he would use on a carpet. His little captive flopped around in protest as Chapman stuck his hands in his pockets and removed his things: a sleek portable phone that folded flat like a wallet, Mrs. Beth Ann Murphy's American Express and Visa cards, three paisley marbles, and a wad of hundred-dollar bills in a gold money clip.

"You jacking me?" the mugger shouted in disbelief. "You a fool."

Chapman thumbed through the thick wad of hundreds. "Why would you rob me with all this?"

"Gimme my shit back!" Kicking the toes of his expensive sneakers against the pavement, the boy rotated himself in jerky moves to face Chapman, who was now clawing around the base of the bank's neatly trimmed hedge. When Chapman found the gun, he stuck it inside his waistband with the butt sticking out. Like a cowboy. A badman.

"You gonna need that," the runt said to Chapman. "You gonna get smoked. I ain't never gonna forget your ugly face."

Chapman thought, that voice! In a movement, he ripped off the abandoned boy's mask, revealing the cursing face of a twelve- or thirteen-year-old boy, but not the boy from the bus, the money counter. This boy was pecan-colored. Two different wads of hundreds, two different boys. Amazing.

He touched the mole on the boy's right cheek, the nose ring, ran his bloody fingers through the haircut like a wiry, inverted soup bowl. Such a handsome boy.

"What you doing? Get your hands off me. Mother fu—"

Chapman fled the parking lot.

The miracle was that the bus arrived before the homeboys returned.

"Don't stare at me!" Chapman told the bus driver and the people riding the bus. He stumbled on, paid his fare with a bill from the money clip, didn't wait for change. Stemming the blood with his shirttail padded against his head, he hunkered down in a seat in the last row. The bus hummed through neglected neighborhoods, came to a stop. He stumbled off. He arrived at his father's door. Knocked.

His father gasped when he saw him. "What happened to you? What did you do to yourself now?"

"Call an ambulance."

"You need Jesus, is what you need."

"Call the ambulance, Daddy!"

He pushed past his father, giddily, steering himself by memory through the hallway to the monochromatic bedroom of his childhood. It was still there. He saw it through the blood. The black sheets, black drapes, black carpet, white desk, white chair, white walls. No mirrors in this entire, crazy house! But the homeboys had his driver license and the key to his apartment. He set the portable phone and the stolen credit cards on the desk. He pulled the wad of money and the gun out of his shirt and pushed them under his mattress. He lay down to sleep away the headache and thought: Vanity.

After his mother had left, the madman said: "No more television, no more meat, no more mirrors. Away with vanity!"—and sent him to school in long sleeves and brogan shoes. Oh, the bullies pummeled him. "Hey, fag. Hey, meatboy. Where'd you get those shoes?" Thoom! He crept through high school. He was a creep. Did he creep! It didn't help that he was thin and had eyes like a girl. He liked his eyes, he couldn't wait to escape. But he was too weak for the streets. A blessing, a curse, Jared took him in. A curse. Jared was a wolf with the ways of a fox. At least it was warm in his house. Jared, approaching from behind, always behind, like a coward: "Don't act like you don't like it. You know you like it." Selling it in the streets to pay Jared back. What was the use of crying? Now there were too many mirrors. Vanity. Vanity. When he slunk back home, the madman said: "Look what you've become." Look what I've become. Look what I am. I am going to kill myself. But he was saved. Love at last, Cricket, with feathers like an angel.

Oh, Cricket.

How did he expect to sleep?

*T*his giddiness.

The police and the paramedics arrived at his father's house at the same time, one party wanting a statement, the other a blood pressure reading. The giddiness turned to dull flatness. Flattening out to black. Noise followed noise. He opened his eyes again under hospital lights.

He has no concussion, he heard someone say. A miracle, his father said. There was a stinging at the base of his neck. He remembered he had toes, and he wiggled them. Someone rubbed a salve over his eye that stiffened the skin. They saw that he was awake and nodded to each other. And prayer, his father said, in answer to something the doctor had said. And Tylenol 3, we'll look at him tonight, but he's strong, he should be good to go tomorrow, the doctor said. Noise followed noise. Chapman went back to sleep. Woke up to a breakfast of oatmeal and a hard-boiled egg. They wheeled him downstairs.

His father met him in the big, white church bus, his father in his tall, black hat, just like the old days, with ashes on his face and hands, as he had been praying all night. "My son, my son," he said, rising from the driver's seat. He positioned himself for embrace, but Chapman gave him a weak handshake instead. He sat way in the back. He hated this bus. He was a boy again, on his way to school just like this. Oh, the bullies were waiting: "Hey, fag. Hey, meatboy!" The old madman in the tall black hat sang: "Jesus, savior, pilot me, over life's tempestuous seas." When Chapman got home, the gun and the more than six thousand dollars were under his mattress were he had hid them. Oh, the bullies vanished.

Oh, the possibilities.

*T*hen again, there was the boy from whom he had stolen the paisley marbles.

Lieutenant Smythe said, "There are too many easy marks out there for them to come after you." Smythe was a jovial man in a tweed jacket, cigarette smoke circling his head like a halo. "They got your money. What do they want you for?"

"They got my driver license," Chapman said. He had spent the week at his father's home. He wore dark glasses to hide the bruises above his eye. He had cut his stylized coif down to a neat crew cut and dyed the tips brick red to complement his undertones. "They got the key to my apartment."

"They got away, is what they got," said the smiling police officer.

"They might want revenge."

"You should be the one seeking revenge," said Lieutenant Smythe, "unless there's some reason they'd come after you. Is there?"

"No," Chapman said. "It's just I saw his face." When Chapman rubbed the toes of his hundred-dollar sneakers together, they squeaked. He was still breaking them in. "That kid swore he'd kill me."

"Was this before or after you tied him up?"

"What do you mean?"

"Did you *do* something to him?" Smythe asked, a comical look spreading across his face. "Come on, you can tell me."

"I didn't *do* anything to him."

Smythe laughed. "Well, he was all tied up. All tied up with no place to go," he sang tunelessly.

Chapman didn't answer. It was a disgusting thing to suggest. I'm the victim here.

With a great push, Lieutenant Smythe rose from his chair. There was an apologetic look on is face, but Chapman didn't think it was genuine. "You can't be too careful, I guess. I apologize. Really." Smythe walked Chapman to the door of his office. He handed Chapman in an unsealed envelope the letter ordering the landlord to release him from the lease agreement. He put a hand on Chapman's shoulder. "But your boys were amateurs. They always make threats. Don't worry yourself about them."

"They make good on their threats, too."

"Only on TV. Check statistics, my friend," Smythe said. "They mostly kill each other. The way I figure, the kid was embarrassed, tough guy like him bound in carpet wire." The police officer laughed and his belly jiggled.

Chapman said, "I'd just feel safer if you had caught them."

"Bad pennies always turn up," Smythe assured.

Chapman rode the elevator down to the first floor. He bought a candy bar from the machine next to the metal detector. He walked through the metal detector, smiling at the uniformed grandfather tending it. Outside, he grinned against the sun. Today's headache was not so strong as yesterday's. He was healing. Then he saw the parking ticket on his windshield.

Chapman picked it up. Maybe Lieutenant Smythe, he thought, can get this excused. He looked up to the lieutenant's fifth-floor window and felt a twinge of nervousness with the smiling police officer looking down on him and his new car.

Then he thought, I bought a car. What does it prove? Besides, he had already figured Smythe for a fool. Chapman waved up at the police officer. Then he cranked down his convertible top and pulled away from the curb.

*C*hapman was changing.

He didn't let customers push him around anymore. Sales picked up. When he threatened to quit the carpet store, Mr. Vangaart promoted him to assistant manager. He warned Jared to stay away from him— "Or I'll break your frigging face"— and Jared hadn't called in a month.

Neither did he let his father drag him through daily prayers though he was living under his roof. But when Chapman brought home a box of KFC, the old man's jaw fell open. "If meat offendeth my brother then I will eat no meat!" He stormed off to his room where he began to pray in his thundering pulpit voice: "I beseech thee, Lord Jesus, give me strength in these last and evil days when children embrace the wickedness of Babylon." He might have prayed all night, but Chapman would never know, for he left the house after midnight. He had decided, at last, to go see Cricket at the place where she worked.

The Co Co Rico was really two night clubs. In one, there was the sixteen-piece live band, the chopped English of the Austrian who introduced the performers, and the lighted stage where the painted folk danced for cheers and dollar bills. This was a tough club, but you'd never know it. Everyone dressed fabulously, and the three burly bouncers, Yves, Gogan, and Hannibal, kept the rowdies in line. The other club, the club within the club, was a cool, dark chamber of cement and cheap exterior paint that changed color from week to week to cover up the explicit messages left by the patrons. It was smoke filled. It was a meeting place. A wooden door, which opened and closed frequently, separated the intimate room from the blatant; if the noise of the first ever became too much, however, there was a grand porch overlooking a service alley that was quite lovely when the moon was out.

The moon was out tonight, and Chapman was out on the porch. He sat at the table farthest from the sliding glass door with his two good friends, Roberto, the mail carrier, and Bing, the brother of Oswald, Cricket's new love. They all wore expensive over-sized Italian shirts and double-pleated leather slacks. Roberto gorged himself on salted pretzel sticks. Bing ordered another round of drinks, and though Bing did not give a reason, Chapman figured it was to celebrate his new prosperity, which amazed them all.

"I've found a little place near Easter Lake," Chapman said. He spoke loud enough for everyone on the porch to hear, even Cricket, feigning contentment at her table near the door with Oswald. With his double chin and his receding hairline, Oswald appeared much older than his thirty-two years. "I move in next week."

"I know a supervisor who lives in Easter Lake," said Roberto. "It's quite exclusive."

"It's not all that," said Chapman, catching Cricket's eye. Cricket smiled. Cricket as yet wore her feathers and paint, although she was finished performing for the night. Perhaps she was still interested. Bing reported that she had inquired about the new car as a matter of fact, but no more than that. Chapman said, "I'm subletting a lean-to, really. One bedroom, one bath, only $250 a month, but the view is absolutely breathtaking."

"For $250 a month?" said Bing. "Even a birdhouse in that area costs twice that."

Chapman laughed. "I'm friendly with the lady who owns the property." This was, of course, Mrs. Beth Ann Murphy, whose credit cards he had rescued.

"But to qualify for a place like that," said Roberto. "The credit check, the deposit…"

"Do we have to talk about this?" Chapman said.

"I think we do," said Roberto, munching pretzels. He pointed with his lips to Cricket and Oswald. "When you lose a catch like that, well, we don't expect to see you enjoying the finer things anytime soon. We expect despair, miserable drunkenness, a suicide attempt."

"Yes," said Bing. "You get mugged. Get knocked so hard in the head your brain rattles, and you come back a big shot. I don't understand it. Maybe I need a good hit in the head."

Chapman laughed, but refused to reveal his secret. It was true he had become more assertive. He couldn't decide whether it was because of the six-thousand-dollar windfall, or the gun he carried always, or the car, the twenty-year-old, eight-cylinder, cherry-red plum. She was worth every penny he had paid for her. She was the kind of car Cricket liked. Big with a strong engine. Chapman decided he was strong too, if not so big. A badman. He said, "Guys, how about a ride?"

"Yes." Roberto and Bing rose immediately to leave.

Chapman rose along with them and said to Bing, "Perhaps your brother and his companion would like to ride with us too."

Oswald heard this, of course. "We're fine right where we are, thank you," he shouted from his table. Moon-faced Cricket shrugged.

Chapman could have left it at that, but he didn't. "But it's no problem, really. It seats six easily, which means Cricket will have to sit on your lap, Oswald, since you take up room enough for three."

Cricket's mouth formed an 'O.' Oswald coughed up wine on his white suit. Roberto made a sound like "whoosh!" and grabbed another handful of pretzels. Bing pulled at Chapman's arm: "Let's get out of here."

But Oswald, assuming the refined voice and unflagging manners of a true gentleman, responded, "Good one." He even dabbed at his mouth delicately with a napkin. "We have our own car, thank you." A Mercedes. Oswald, the high-school drop out, had muscled his way into management at an accounting firm. He lifted his drink as in a toast. "—although I rarely pass up an opportunity to have Cricket sit on my lap."

Chapman raised a fist. "You fat toad—"

"Anytime you're ready, carpet boy," said Oswald, the gangster, pushing away from the table, rising to legs stout as tree trunks.

Cricket clung to Oswald, trying to restrain him. Hannibal the bouncer, who had once tossed a rowdy from the porch into the alley three floors below, mashed out his cigarette in a shot glass and faced the commotion. He folded his arms across his barrel of a chest. He was unhappy. He had come out here to catch a breather, and now this. Bing and Roberto pulled Chapman through the glass doors to safety. They forced him into a chair.

"You've had too much to drink," said Bing.

"Are you nuts?" said Roberto, spitting crumbs.

Chapman said, "I can't take it anymore. He stole Cricket."

"So?" said Bing. "Oswald's connected. Hannibal's crazy. You want to get your head bashed in for real?"

"You come back a better man," said Chapman.

"What?" said Roberto, touching the bulge under Chapman's shirt. "And what's this?"

"My frigging gun," said Chapman. Roberto and Bing pulled away from him. "I'm tired of being pushed around."

Of course, Roberto and Bing didn't understand. Roberto the mail carrier did not mace the dogs that harassed him on his route. He sent postcards to their owners, reminding them of the leash law. Bing, who held a bachelor's degree in history, lived in a small room back of his brother Oswald's house and served as his valet and gopher. Oswald kept him in line with "See what I've accomplished with no education? I'm the dumb one and you the brain, but see?" And he, Chapman, the effeminate one, was everyone's punching bag. But not anymore.

Chapman's friends left the table, and he found himself humming the melody seeping in from outside. It was the live band's bump and grind version of "Misty." It wasn't very good. He ordered a gin and tonic. It was brought to him by the one called Widow, who only performed on slow nights, or when someone better called in sick. He gave Widow a large tip because she was better than she thought she was. Only when the lights were too bright could you see how Widow's face was too harsh, her hips too narrow. She was no Cricket, that's for sure. But Widow was better than she thought. Everyone was better!

Jared, dressed as Mae West, approached his table.

Chapman raised the gun. "Slide off!"

Jared hiked up his skirts and fled.

"That's right," said Chapman, who was not as drunk as he behaved. "I'm wait-ing for you, Oswald." There was only one way in from the porch. He watched the glassed exit. He ordered another gin and tonic.

A hand seized Chapman's neck from behind. He reached for his gun, but there was a hand at his waist already jerking the gun from inside his belt. Hannibal pulled Chapman up from his chair.

"We don't allow this here," Hannibal said, pressing the gun against Chapman's nose.

"Wait," said Chapman.

Hannibal, who had forearms like the buttocks of a bull, dragged Chapman through a service door, down three flights of stairs, through a brightly lit kitchen (where two men in jeans and sandals rolled dough and stirred a pot of something redolent of garlic), through a hallway the Co Co Rico shared with a dentist's clinic, a hobby shop, and a hair salon, then tossed him through the steel door onto the rain-slicked ground of the service alley.

Hannibal held up the gun. "You bring this in here once, you ain't never allowed back."

"Let me explain," said Chapman, climbing to his knees. His shirt was torn and soaked with the reeking fluid from the alley floor.

"Don't come back," said the bouncer. "This ain't that kind of joint."

"That's what you say." Chapman was back on his feet. Oswald was a gangster. The painted people could be had for ten dollars. The live band lived on dope. It *was* that kind of joint. "At least give me my piece back," he said.

"Your piece." Hannibal plucked the sleeve of ammunition from the gun and tossed it east, and then the gun west. Chapman noted the location of their fall. He moved to retrieve the gun first. Then Hannibal said, "She say she want to go for a ride."

"What?"

"She say she want to go for a ride," Hannibal said. "Meet her in an hour at the carpet store. She say you seem to got your act together."

Chapman raised his hands in victory. "Thank you," he said.

"Just don't come back here," said Hannibal. "Never, ever." He lumbered back inside and closed the heavy, steel door.

Chapman drove to an all-night gas station. He filled the tank because he anticipated a lot of driving. Anywhere Cricket wanted to go, he'd take her. He got the bathroom key chained to a lead pipe from the attendant in exchange for his car keys and washed his face and hands. Then he wasted ten minutes trying to wash the stinky smell out of his Italian shirt with hand soap from the drippy dispenser and cold water from the tap. He returned the bathroom key and pipe. For fifteen dollars and ninety-nine cents, he purchased a black T-shirt that said "Welcome To My World." He slipped it over his head. The attendant, a scratchy woman, said through the speaker in the bulletproof glass, "Don't you look grand?" She swung his change to him on a silver tray on the steel-mesh carousel.

When Chapman got to the Rug Emporium, he noticed right away something was wrong. The door to the store was rolled open. Several rugs were flung here and there about the parking lot. Another car, an old warhorse Buick, its trunk overflowing with throw rugs, was parked beside Cricket's Chevy. "Jesus," Chapman said under his breath.

When he cut his engine, he heard the sounds of the struggle coming from behind the big green dumpster.

"Punk! Bitch!"

He gripped the gun. As he passed the Buick, he noted the broken rear window on the driver's side. The gun was heavy in his hand, and human life was precious, but those brats, as Lieutenant Smythe called them, had followed him. They wanted their money back. They wanted their gun.

The sounds were Thoom! Thoom! Then a groan followed by boyish laughter. Thoom!

"Cricket," Chapman breathed.

Chapman dashed around the dumpster, catching the three men wearing stocking masks completely by surprise. He ran up to the shortest thug, who as he guessed was the one doing the beating, and pumped three shots into his back. Crack! Crack! Crack! Fire poured from Chapman's fingers.

The short boy's companions fled at the report of the shots echoing off the concrete walls. One boy hopped the small fence back where the Mexican restaurant used to be. The tall one slipped around the other side of the dumpster, and his footfalls padded rapidly into silence.

What surprised Chapman was that the one he had shot, the short one, had collapsed on top of what turned out to be the prone body of a badly beaten Oswald. "Thank God. Thank God," Oswald said, pushing the limp body of the fallen boy away from him.

"What are you doing here?" Chapman pointed the gun at him.

"Thank God. These punks came out of nowhere."

"Where's Cricket?"

"I owe you," Oswald said. He sat up. He indicated the dead boy with a nod, his little hand still clutching his gun. "We've got to get out of here before the police come."

Chapman heard the sirens, too. He still had the gun trained on Oswald. "It was you who gave Hannibal that message. You were going to kill me."

Oswald put up his hands. "It was stupid jealousy. But I owe you now. I pay my bills."

"Cricket doesn't love me."

"You know how it is with that kind. The more macho the man, the more like a woman she feels." Oswald winked. "She would really like you now."

"I could shoot you and say the dead boy did it, you fat toad!"

"Good one. Very funny." Oswald was on his feet now, his white suit slick with rain and the dead boy's blood. "Put that gun away before you get yourself in real trouble, Chapman. I'll call some of my people and take care of this."

"I could shoot—"

"Put it away," Oswald said.

Chapman wanted very much to shoot Oswald, but already there were the flashing lights of police vehicles behind him.

*C*hapman's chest heaved. He covered his face with his hands.

"Don't go all to pieces, buddy," Smythe said. "He was a punk. You probably won't even get charged."

"You don't understand how this changes everything," said Chapman. Cricket didn't love him or his car. The police had taken his gun. Oswald had given a statement that implied they were, well, friends. Horrible. "I'm no better now than—"

"You're much better than this little punk," said Smythe, not understanding that what Chapman wanted to say was that he was not much better now than he was before the jack-move at the ATM. Smythe said, "He was street trash. You're a decent, hardworking fellow who defended himself the only way he could."

"It is an awful life," said Chapman, but maybe Smythe was right. "I did to him what he tried to do to me. Yes."

"Shhh…" Smythe walked over to the little body, surrounded now by paramedics and an officer with plastic gloves and a camera. "You did the world a favor." He pulled the stocking mask off the boy and lifted the face for Chapman to see. "You were right. We should have listened. Same bad penny, right? He followed you here, attacked your, ahem, friend." Smythe glanced at Oswald leaning against a squad car, smoking a cigarette and weeping frantically, and suppressed another belly laugh. Smythe said about the dead boy, "Well, he got just what he deserved. Good riddance."

Chapman sat down on the ground, not caring that he might damage his leather pants. He hugged his knees. That face! This punk was not the boy with the paisley marbles. This one was coffee-skinned and bald. Two different jack-moves, two different boys.

Oh, Cricket, he thought. Oh, Cricket. What an awful world. And this one is the spitting image of you.

Prince William Blows GOOD

William and Esther got married after a difficult courtship.

Esther's parents, a wealthy doctor and his socialite wife, did not approve of William because he was, in their words, "shiftless and exhibited the worst qualities of our much-maligned race." When they met him, William was three years out of the army, unemployed, and lacked any ambition towards continuing his education, though he had graduated near the top of his high-school class and was well read. William's friends were mostly boozers and gamblers, and while William was not much of a drinker himself, he spent way too much time at the track. William played the dogs and the horses, but he did not play them well—at least not as well as he played the blues on his tenor saxophone a few nights a week at a club owned by Packard, a chip-toothed ex-con who just happened to be William's uncle and the only family he had ever known. William played the blues: the music of sadness, grief, and heartache. And he played them good.

No, Esther's parents did not approve of William, not at all, but Esther, after hearing him blow just once, thought William was the beginning and the end of the world. Such is youth and a young girl's fancy.

When William blew, he blew hard.

A premed senior on summer break from Princeton, Esther found herself giving to the dashing young William the prize she had guarded all her life so as to present it to her husband unblemished on their wedding night. Her passion was such that poor William soon found himself smaller than Esther's impression of him, and he had to stretch long and hard to measure up. William pulled out his horn. He blew hard. He blew good. He blew so good that the door opened and the cool air rushed in, chasing the stuffiness out of the room. Strangers gathered in the hallway of the cheap hotel to listen and breathe.

"It must be love," Esther told him, trembling under the sheets, as somewhere else her mother was crying, and in a nearby room her father was putting bullets in a rather large handgun and having visions of William and himself facing off in a dark and mythic alley. There would be no graduation from Princeton in the happy spring, for there was the terrible bluesman leading their child astray. But neither would there be a fatal show-down in the dank alley, or even a bribe to keep him away from her, for as always there was a baby, coming like a sprite from the bowels of hell, to bind that which should never be bound.

They named her Gale, for when her father blew, he blew hard and he blew good. And now, with Gale and Esther in his care, William blew more often, for he was not happy taking money from the wealthy in-laws who had stood so firmly against him.

"We'll show them," William told Esther, and then went out to blow at a gig that didn't pay enough to cover their bills even when added to the money Esther made as a teacher's aide.

"It's his pride," Esther told her mother and her father.

"Take the money, baby," her parents told her.

"I can't," Esther told them.

"Think about little Gale," they told her, and Esther took the money from them, time and time again. For little Gale.

Winters are cold in Newark, and playing the blues doesn't pay well. But bluesmen know about passion, and William had this and more for his daughter, even when less than a year into the marriage he had begun to turn cool towards Esther. William blew for Gale, and she responded with a gurgle from deep in her infant chest, a sound that was on key, a sound that was harmonic, an approving sound. When William was around, no one could get near Gale. William fed Gale, William bathed Gale, William changed Gale when she needed changing, this last giving him a peculiar kind of thrill because far up on the babe's right inner thigh was a birthmark that William took as a sign the child was his especially. A birthmark in the shape of a saxophone.

"See how it curves here," William said, when Esther argued that the mark looked more like the letter 'S' than a saxophone. "But notice it stops short at the top. That's the mouthpiece."

"I guess it could be," said Esther. "I guess." It hurt Esther that William no longer blew for her—not a single note—after she had given up so much for him. Esther knew William was romantically involved with the woman who occasionally sang with him at Packard's club—Libby. Esther knew that if not for the precious little Gale he would leave her for Libby, the floozy. Men are like that, especially bluesmen. They want a woman who can more than swoon to their music; they want a woman who understands the notes. But Gale was her insurance.

Thus, when Gale was kidnapped from the little nursery where she had been taken for just a few short weeks so that Esther could attend classes in a special program of study Rutgers was offering for mothers returning to school, Esther prayed for a miracle, but none came. Only ransom notes written on postcards from assorted topless bars in New Mexico.

Esther's parents put the fifty thousand dollars in a shopping bag and William put the bag in the second of three phone booths outside the Greyhound bus terminal and a police officer dressed in rags and pushing a shopping cart full of plastic bottles watched the money in the bag in the phone booth for five days. No one came, and the ransom notes stopped.

"They knew he was a cop," William said.

"Oh," said Esther, trembling.

"They killed my Gale."

"My baby," said Esther.

"Gale," William said, and he took out his horn.

William had never blown so good, so blue.

It's funny how misfortune turns on fortune—the bad thing becoming good—when you flip it over. Not that William ever considered Gale's kidnapping a good thing, but it wasn't long after that his fame reached beyond his Uncle Packard's night club and got the attention of an Atlantic City record producer, "Happy" Buddy Jordan, who was looking for just such a sound as proceeded from the bell of the sax that William blew. Happy Jordan built a quartet around William's saxophone and began calling him "Prince William" and their sweet partnership produced three very popular albums: Prince William's Stormy Gale; Gale Force; and Dare the Gales Blow.

The money Prince William earned from the albums was more than he could ever lose at the dog or horse track. The money put him on an equal footing with his in-laws, and his mood improved. Esther, though, worried that the WOMAN, Libby, who sang no fewer than three cuts on each of her husband's albums, was becoming all too brazen. Libby accompanied him to all club dates and blues festivals, even when she was not scheduled to sing. When Esther came along, Libby slept in an adjoining room. Esther little doubted that Libby and her bluesman shared a room when she, his lawful wife, stayed at home. Brazen Libby introduced herself as Esther's friend.

"I'm his wife's best friend," she told beat reporters when they asked, and then she threw an arm around Prince William and laughed. "I'm here to keep all those naughty girls away from him."

Esther ignored her parents' advice—divorce him—because his was, as yet, the only horn that had ever blown for her.

It ended, however, with the fourth album, Blow Gales Blow, an album which was not nearly so good as its predecessors. Prince William's blowing was but a memory of its former self. But that album was his biggest seller ever and earned him a Grammy nomination for the cut "My Lost Girl," which blues historians were later to call "the only hot moment on a lukewarm piece of wax." Prince William dedicated the album to "Libby, My Wife's Best Friend." Shortly thereafter Esther sued for divorce, won the better part of the money, and moved back with her parents, under whose encouragement she completed her education and became a high-school science teacher with a reputation for being tough.

To his credit, Prince William had, in fact, dedicated the first three albums to "My Devoted Wife, Esther."

Libby and Prince William married four days after his divorce with Esther was finalized. The union of Libby and Prince William lasted a long time but was less than fruitful. Libby became pregnant four times—three boys and a girl—and each time lost the child early in the third trimester. She had, it turned out, a weak birth canal. They never made much money. Together, Libby and Prince William produced a pair of less-than-successful albums and then decided to work independently: She went back to singing at nightclubs; he continued turning out albums with his quartet, a few of which were popular but never so much as his earlier attempts. The critics often referred to him as being past his prime, and he realized they were right. Somehow and somewhere along the way he had forgotten how to blow his horn.

Libby stayed with Prince William though he grew sullen and mean and fed what little money they made to the dogs and the horses. Such is a woman's plight. How can she walk away when her bluesman blows for her, long, hard, and quite often good? Blows the diamond wedding band right off the third finger of her left hand and turns it into what he can get for it in cash—eight hundred seventy-one dollars and no small change, which to Prince William was another sign. Eight. Seven. One. He had dreamt them just like that, too. Eight. Seven. One. But just to be sure, he played them every way possible in every race. And when they came in, they came in big, so Prince William bought Libby a fancy hat shaped like a bell and a mink coat straight from Russia.

Wearing the hat, the coat, and nothing else, Libby followed his lilting notes from one end of the bed to the other. She had never been so happy—because now he, for a change, was happy.

Then she said, "What about the ring, baby?"

"Pawn man sold it," Prince William said, slipping the horn to his lips.

"Oh no," she said. "That was my momma's ring."

"I'll buy you another ring," he said.

"Oh no," Libby said, looking at her naked hand. "Oh no."

The room smelled of Chanel No. 5 and raspberry incense and sweat, and it trembled with the force of Prince William's blowing. Libby, her back to him now, tried to quell her sobs with a cigarette, but she began to cough and choke, so she put it out. Libby loved her bluesman that much.

Eighteen years after Prince William married her, Libby died of lung cancer. Esther sent a bouquet of African violets draped with a scarlet ribbon with a card addressed to "My Best Friend's Husband," but Prince William did not open it. A week later, Prince William's Uncle Packard died in a car crash. Esther sent no flowers that he knew of, but then again he didn't stay long at the funeral. They all die, his mind wailed. Libby. Packard. Gale. Such a sadness overwhelmed him that he went home to consider ending his own life.

Instead, of course, he picked up his horn and blew as he hadn't blown in years, for that's what the blues is: the musical expression of sadness, grief, and heartache.

Prince William blew, and he blew good, and, finally, the thing that was missing for so long returned to him—passion. He found her in Happy Jordan's studio. She was just about half Prince William's age and trying to make it as a blues singer. She called herself Ruth and claimed she learned the blues growing up "divorced from the quality of life in an East Orange, New Jersey, orphanage." Happy Jordan had his doubts about her ability, but Prince William found her to be pretty and, too, there was something primal about her voice. He asked her to work out with his quartet on some of the tunes Libby used to sing, the ones that had left no doubt in Esther's mind about what was going on between the floozy singer and her bluesman husband.

Ruth sang. No, she couldn't growl the low notes like Libby used to so that you felt like "trading your pride and your seat at the bar for another lousy night with the one who done you wrong," but she was always on key and she could improvise considerably in spite of her limited range. The blues was in her blood.

"She's no Libby," said Happy Jordan.

"True," Prince William said. "But she sings the note I like, over and over again."

Happy Jordan looked at the pretty woman practicing scales with the piano player; he looked again at Prince William who had somehow regained his form. He warned, "Remember, Prince William, we're not so young as we used to be."

"True," the bluesman said, and then he blew and blew until Ruth plucked the mouthpiece from his mouth and kissed his skillful lips one half inch at a time.

"I must be gentle," she said. "Your mouth is your money."

"You are the only woman I ever truly desired."

"Why desire that which you already possess?"

"Exactly what I mean. I have you and I want you yet."

"How deep is your want?"

"Infinite."

"Take me," Ruth said, and without shifting his body on the bed, Prince William did just that.

Sex with Ruth was harmonic. She made him feel young again, but not really

young, for when he was young he was foolish, and there was certainly nothing foolish about their lovemaking. No, Ruth did not make Prince William *feel* young. She
was his youthful vigor made flesh. She was his muse. As they rocked back and
forth, songs came to his lips and Ruth completed the lyrical motif. He moaned the
tune, she screamed the words. Their orgasm was a coda. "Ruth understood his
notes," Esther would have said.

Ruth was perfect. With her, Prince William little doubted his next album
would be his best.

"You complete me," he said.

"It feels so natural working—and being—with you," she said.

"It seems I've desired you all of my life," he said.

"It seems I've known you all my life," she said. "I listened to your *Gale* albums
in the orphanage. Every song you played seemed dedicated to me."

"That was a black period in my life. I'm glad you didn't commit suicide," he
said. "What kind of orphanage plays the blues?"

"I had special treatment." Her little hand uncoiled the hairs on his chest one at
a time. "My parents were dead, but an elderly couple—their distant relations, they
claimed—took an interest in me. Their generosity ensured I was clothed and fed
better than the other kids. They hired tutors for me so that I was better educated,
too. They wrote me comforting letters, sent me toys, sent me makeup and toiletries,
gifts at Christmas, paid for singing lessons—and they sent me every album you ever
made." Her words undid his heart.

"Did you ever meet this couple?" he said, turning away from her in the dark,
feeling around for his horn. "Did they ever visit?"

"Yes, often. And now I visit them all the time."

"And?" he said. He found his mouthpiece. He slipped a new reed into place
without seeing.

"You guessed it," she said. "They look so much like me. I just know they are my
parents . . . even though they deny it. I have the old man's eyes. The old woman's
complexion."

She was right. Prince William saw her face in the impenetrable darkness. The
eyes, the complexion were his in-laws'. So was the broad forehead. The lips were
Esther's; Esther's breasts. The music, though, was his. How, God, had he missed the
music? The strange, dark harmony rising, as it were, from the bowels of hell to bind
that which should never be bound? They had tricked him, the old fools. Tricked
their own daughter too. To break up a marriage that was doomed anyway.

Prince William blew.

"I'm their child, and I don't know why they deny me. But that's why I sing the
blues," Ruth said.

Prince William blew hard, the pulse of his music in syncopation with the beat of his heart. And then Prince William turned on the light, for he had to be certain. He had to know for sure. The birthmark, the small saxophone on her right inner thigh: was that there too?

"It's an 'S'," Ruth said. "An 'S' for singer."

"It's a saxophone," Prince William said, because it was.

Prince William and Ruth did not make love again that night. When he was certain she was asleep, he arose quietly, packed up his horn, and kissed her forehead. He drove to the old doctor's house and sat on the porch in the love seat just outside the front door. He had a loaded gun under his coat. Who would suffer more, he wondered, if he killed them? After a while, he took out his saxophone and interpreted the music pounding to be let out of his head. The lights blinked on, and his ex-father-in-law's face peered through the window. Prince William blew and he blew hard, but it was complex stuff, more jazz than blues, and he soon lost interest in playing and left, which was certainly a lucky break for the old doctor.

Prince William caught a Greyhound to Miami, where he swapped his saxophone at a pawn shop for a lawnmower and hired himself out as a yardman. He planted pretty flowers, and it made him happy to see them in full bloom. He practiced hard and became expert at sculpting hedges. He sculpted animals mostly: deer, rabbits, a few fast dogs now and again.

◆ ◆ ◆

Prince William has changed his name to Ed, and Ed owns both the albums Ruth has put out. They are his most prized possessions. Of course, Ed hasn't listened to Ruth's albums—and he never will. As a rule he no longer plays the blues, his or anybody's.

Ed has heard that they aren't very good albums anyway. The critics call Ruth a "shallow, faint talent who has no business singing the blues."

Ed doesn't know if Ruth's lack of success is such a bad thing, however. The blues is, after all, the music of sadness, grief, and heartache.

"At least I spared her that," Ed says.

The Lord of Travel

The next customer is a real lay down.

She rides in on a bike. It's like she has "Scholarship Money" stamped on her forehead. I run in order to get to her before Curly or the Arab can.

"My name is Ida," she says, taking my hand.

I love the way you speak, Ida. Where are you from?

"I'm from New Jersey," she says.

New Jersey, I say.

This New Jersey joke runs through my brain—something about the "Garbage" State Bridge—but I can't remember the punch line. It's just as well. If I offend her, I'll have a harder time selling her the car. So I play up the tough Northerner thing.

Oh yes, the South sucks. Too slow. Not like up North, I say (although the farthest north I've ever been is Gainesville). Not like New Jersey. Only one thing would make a sane person leave New Jersey for a one horse town like Miami. You're a student.

"Yes. U.M. How did you guess?"

Glasses, looking intelligent but stunning on your pretty face. You rode a bike. And I don't see your father, husband, or boyfriend. All independent women in this town are students or lawyers.

When Ida laughs, her teeth show even and white. Her laugh says she likes me, trusts me. I have sold myself well. If this keeps up, she's going to drive home in a brand new clunker and they'll need a wheelbarrow to deliver my paycheck.

I run a hand over the shiny parts of the car and begin my spiel.

Beautiful finish, I say. One owner, I claim. Great gas mileage, I lie, for a car this size. Four-door convenience—just right for someone with a lot of friends. I myself took this baby to the beach last week (just don't tell my manager, ha-ha-ha), and girl, let me tell you how they envied me. A true classic, only ten thousand were made.

She notices a door handle is missing.

That little thing can be fixed, I say. Oh yes, we were going to fix that anyway. Don't you worry about that.

She runs a hand along the scratched up left side.

And those scratches? We can paint those. Here, let me write it down. Scratches . . . Door handle . . . . Anything else? OK. Back tires, side view mirror, dent in roof. Good, good. We'll take care of everything, really.

She turns to eye other cars on the lot. Resistance.

Ida, I say, touching her hand, making Honest Abe eye contact. Ida, for the kind of money you're looking to spend, this is the best buy in town. The absolutely best buy. True, I could show you something a bit nicer, a little cleaner, but you'd have to raise your sights. Over there, for instance—the red Mustang. Pretty, isn't it? I'd love to sell it to you, but you're talking at least four thousand dollars more. Can you do that?

"No."

I didn't think so. You see, Ida, I'm not the kind of guy who is going to rip off a young, attractive sister like yourself. Especially with you being in school. I was a student, and I know what it's like to live on a budget. Plus, you might become a lawyer one day and sue the hell out of me.

"That's right," she laughs.

I laugh.

Black people have to stick together, I say, opening the car door.

I take her for a test ride, and she begins to act more and more like a buyer. She adjusts her seat and the rearview mirror to her comfort. She fiddles with the radio. She plays with the knobs on the dashboard until she figures out the air conditioner. Cool air rushes out of the vents, humming. For my part, I am pleased that the car doesn't stall in neutral as it did the day before.

All the while I'm saying, Nice car, Isn't it? Drives great, doesn't it? Air feels good, doesn't it?

And I watch her head nod in approval. I am putting Ida in a "yes" mood. After saying "yes" twenty times, it's hard to say "no." Psychology.

Ida turns down a lonely street and punches the accelerator. The car belches forward, its ancient V-8 roaring mightily, "Out of my way! I am the Lord of Travel, master of the road!" Blue-gray smoke trails out of the exhaust pipes, but Ida doesn't notice. She is a woman in love with a car. She smiles all the way back to the lot.

We park.

Ida sucks in a deep breath. When she turns to face me, her smile is replaced by a look of false concern. She is about to pretend she is little interested in the car so that she can get a better deal from me. She will claim she can't afford it, say she needs to think about it, say she is considering other cars, say she wants her father, husband, boyfriend to look at it before she decides. She will try very hard to get the best possible deal, and she will fail utterly. However valiant be her fight, she is out-matched. You see, Ida is buying her first car; I sell them every day.

You felt good in that car, didn't you?

I nod my head. She nods hers.

It drove so sweetly, didn't it?

I nod my head. She nods hers.

If you could get a good deal on this car, you'd buy it, wouldn't you?

I nod my head. She nods hers—and then she shakes it, saying, "But I don't know how much it costs."

Ida, did I mention cost? Listen to me carefully. If I write a deal that you, IDA, feel is the best deal in the world on this wonderful car that you, IDA, are in love with, would you, IDA, buy the car and drive it home today?

I nod my head. She nods hers. "Yes, if you did all those things. Yes," Ida commits. Ida is a real lay down, the customer who buys it just the way you lay it out—

no questions, no resistance, just an occasional burst of delighted giggling.

We go inside and she signs her name to various documents that give her title to the over-priced gas guzzler. She writes the dealership a check. I hand her the keys. She drives off.

Done deal.

The others come over and pat me on the back to hide their envy. They ask how much money I made.

Too much, I tell them.

The manager shakes my hand. Biggest sale of the month on a car he thought no one would sell, the Lord of Travel—a wreck on wheels, a bone mobile, a junker, a heap. And to sell it as though it were the best car on the lot! He mentions a bonus. What wouldn't he do for the guy who just bought him another month or two in his cushy job?

Then Ida returns.

I see her through the glass doors, walking briskly. She seems irritated. I suspect she is suffering from buyer's remorse, the headache buyers get when they drive off the lot and begin to realize that they didn't get such a sweet deal after all.

The others move away from me, eyebrows raised. Oh-oh, they think. Another sale gone sideways. Customer wants her money back.

I suspect they are right.

Ida says, "You forgot to give me one of those temporary tags."

(Praise God.)

No problem, I say. Wouldn't want you to get a ticket.

I make out the tag, the magic marker shaking in my grasp. I tape it to her rear windshield. I congratulate her again on her wise purchase, and she hugs me, of all things.

"I feel so independent now," she says.

The car coughs, rattles, emits black smoke, and finally starts. Ida smiles stupidly and drives off. She even waves good-bye.

Yes, a real lay down.

$ $ $

I go inside. I am a nervous wreck. My palms are sweating. I make for the bathroom but can't get past Curly and the Arab, who block my path.

Curly says, "Close call."

Never doubted it for a second, I say.

The Arab says, "I had a customer like that once. Easy sale. Full pop. A real lay down. He leaves the store, right? I'm celebrating when I get this phone call. It's raining and I had forgotten to show the guy how to work his wipers. So I explain it to him over the phone and we hang up. Half hour later, this guy shows up, and he is pissed. The windshield wipers work fine, but the car stalls when he turns 'em on. Get it? So he can't drive in the rain. He can't have the wipers and the engine on at the same time."

Curly laughs. "I remember that car. Twenty-dollar paint job covered up all the rust. Came this close to selling it to a missionary when it conked out."

"That's the car, that's the car," says the Arab, who hates being interrupted. "So I tell this guy to bring the car back tomorrow so's the mechanic can look at. The wires are crossed or something. No. He wants it done now or he wants his money back. We go back and forth like this. But you know me. I finally tell him to make like Michael Jackson and *Beat It!* He starts to cuss and scare off the other customers, and he wants to sue . . ."

The Arab drones on. I hardly listen, but I nod in the right places. I know this story. I've been involved in hundreds like it. As Curly winds up to tell his version of the same tale, I steal away to the bathroom where I dry my palms and my forehead.

What is wrong with me?

Checking the mirror, I notice my tie hangs funny, and there is a grimy spot where my gold tie pin would be if I had not hocked it. I need a haircut. Once again I forgot to shave. Otherwise, I look great.

So what is wrong with me?

I am sweating. My stomach is jumping. Is it Ida? Is it guilt? No, I am a salesman; I'm hardcore.

A while ago, I closed a phone deal with a local millionaire. Like many wealthy people, he was above coming to the dealership, so I had to go to his house to deliver the car and pick up the check. When he saw that I was black, he revealed himself as a bigot. At his request, I sat in the back during the test drive. When we got back to his home, he did not offer me a seat. I stood while he read through the papers. He even let fly a comment about the damned niggers and spics who are ruining this country. I was unmoved. I told him I was offering him a great car at a great price; he signed the papers and bought the car. I felt a burning hatred for the man, but no guilt for selling him a car. Money is green and silver and copper and gold, never black and white.

When I leave the bathroom, I find Ida waiting in the showroom. Behind her, through the glass walls, I see her car, the Lord of Travel. Its hood is popped open. Thick black smoke is billowing out of the oil pan, and water is spraying up from the radiator.

$ $ $

Well, Ida, I say, it's your car. You chose it. You paid for it.

"Yes, but you said . . . ," she begins.

It's your car. You paid for it.

She considers this silently.

I wait for her to attack me, threaten to sue, or burst into tears. I've seen it all before. Instead she turns away from me and stares at her smoking car. "Great Deal" is still written on the front windshield in large, red letters. The handle bar and front tire of her bike lean out of the half-closed trunk. I deny my need to help her; I must be firm. It is important that she understand it is *her* car polluting the air with smoke and rusty water. No deposit. No return.

When she does turn on me, she is well composed. "I'll stop payment on the check," she says.

It has already been cashed, I tell her.

At our dealership, we "hammer" checks. In other words, we send a runner to cash the check at the issuing bank as soon as we receive it. Ida's check was cashed before she had driven off the lot the first time.

"I'll call a lawyer," she says.

So will we, I say. Now let's see, you were eighteen when you read and then signed the buyer's order, right?

"I trusted you," she says.

You chose the car. You signed for it. Now, if you want our mechanic to look at it, say so and I'll get him to check it out for you tomorrow. If not, you'd better call a towing company to haul it off our lot, or the manager will charge you $50 per day for storage.

Ida wears a white coverall that hangs to mid-thigh, and a light breeze flaps the material around her chubby legs. Flap, flap, flap. Black and smooth is her skin, but at times the loose cloth around her shoulders shifts to reveal a frilly bra strap and the lighter flesh beneath it. Her hands balled into fists are useless on her hips. When her eyes fill up and turn red, I notice something else about Ida, something I didn't notice before.

I am surprised—disturbed by it.

"How much will your mechanic charge?" She says.

If you're nice about it, nothing. Just parts and labor and taxes.

As though there is anything left to charge.

And I'll have Miguel, the lot boy, drive you home in his pickup. I don't want you riding that bike home. It's getting dark. Give me your keys.

Taking her keys, I touch her hand. I linger. I pull away.

As a car salesman, I meet many women I could happily fall in love with, but I usually realize this after I have sold them cars, and then it is too late. The smart ones never want to see me again. And the dumb ones, well, I don't call them back after sex. I just can't respect anyone dumb enough to get screwed twice by the same guy.

It isn't really a bad car, I say. Once we fix it up, you'll see you made a wise purchase.

"OK," she says, "but promise me." Now she is on the verge of tears. I let her take my hand.

Trust me, I say.

"Promise me," she says.

Trust me.

I nod my head.

She nods hers.

"I do trust you," she says, my cold hand warm in both of hers. "You're not like the rest of them."

No, I'm not, I say.

What I notice is, the resemblance is amazing. They are sisters in sadness, Ida and Elaine, the one lost to me forever.

When Miguel returns and they pull off the lot, Ida waves at me. She actually waves at me and smiles, this woman.

And it comes back to me: "Love. God is Love."

$ $ $

It is late.

Outside, the lot boys are locking the doors on all the cars. The security guard, having already blocked off two of the entrances, waits at the third. He checks his watch.

Inside, I watch the Arab dramatize his defeat by throwing up his hands. His customer, a tall, thin man in a white shirt and dress slacks, rises from his chair. The man wears no watch.

"I'm leaving," the man says. "I would like my money and my driver's license back."

The Arab says, "I'll call the manager." He moves towards the man in the white shirt and dress slacks. "Maybe we can work something out." He touches the man's shoulder as though they are old friends, and the man shrinks away.

The man says in a firm voice: "Please, young man, retrieve my money and my license. I no longer wish to do business with you."

"OK, OK," says the Arab, making his way to the tower, where Curly, the manager, and I are waiting. "OK. OK."

The Arab needs a "Turn"—a fresh salesman to save the sale. This is quite a surprise, for the Arab is our best closer.

"He's a puke," the Arab says. He falls heavily into a swivel chair and swivels. "He's not buying. Throw him out on his ass."

The manager counts the man's deposit, four hundred fifty dollars in twenties and tens. He picks up the man's license and turns to me and Curly. "There's still money on the table. Who wants to play manager?"

Curly and I say "I do" at the same time.

"He's a puke, I tell you," insists the Arab.

But Curly and I feel no pressure taking a turn from the dealership's top earner. If we close a deal that has slipped from the Arab's stubborn grasp, then we are super salesmen and we get half the money. If we don't close it, no problem—we weren't expected to anyway. We go home early.

"Give it to me," says Curly to me, "I haven't had a sale in two days."

Yes, I say, but I haven't lost a sale in a week.

Big Curly puts himself between me and the manager. "You owe me one," says Curly to the manager. "I can close this guy. I do well with clean-cut guys."

But preachers are my specialty, I say.

"A preacher," says my manager, handing me the money and the license: Hezekiah McBride, 45, safe driver, most likely a Holy Roller. "Go make us some more money."

"A puke," says the Arab.

I step down from the tower and walk toward Hezekiah McBride. Brother McBride. Pastor McBride. A man whose diction speaks of sterling credit and a *Holy Bible With Concordance* in his briefcase. The good Rev. McBride is not here to play games with heathen who call God "Allah." He's here to buy a car, and I'm just the Sunday school dropout to sell it to him.

So I take my time. I check the tires on our showroom model. I take a side trip into an empty office and sit in the dark for thirty seconds. I come out and sip water from the fountain. I address Miguel who is now pushing a dust mop over the showroom floor. I ask him if he is certain all the cars outside are locked up. When he informs me they are, I say "good" in my most authoritarian baritone and then sip from the fountain again.

I take my time not because I'm afraid of Hezekiah McBride, but because I have his license and his money, which he won't leave without. A power game. The longer a buyer stays in the store—no matter how badly you treat him—the more likely it is he will buy.

Hezekiah McBride demands his money and license as soon as I arrive, ignoring my hand extended for an introductory shake; I hand everything over but position myself at the exit of the half-office so that he cannot leave without pushing past me impolitely. He fumbles to replace his license and money in his fat wallet. In the process, he drops two twenties; I pick them up, hand them to him.

"Thanks," he says.

Hezekiah McBride, because he is a man of God, hopes to conceal his anger. I shall use this against him.

Hezekiah, I say, I could hear your voice way up in the management tower, and, well, we've been having some trouble with him.

I point in the general direction of the Arab.

"That young man is a liar and a thief," he says. "He lied about what he was going to give me for my trade-in until I got ready to sign the papers."

Did he now?

"He said he'd give me a thousand, but then he added the cost of air and tires and rust proofing to the new car, raising its price by seven hundred fifty."

In effect, paying you two hundred fifty dollars for your trade-in.

"Two hundred fifty dollars."

I frown. I pick up the buyer's order.

Is this the deal?

"Yes."

Trading in a '74 Eldorado. Moderate condition . . .

"Good condition," he corrects. "It just had a paint job."

. . . Some rust. Missing grille. Bald tires. Forty-two thousand miles.

"Two hundred forty-two thousand," he says. "It went over twice."

Thanks for being so honest.

"Mine is not a deceitful tongue."

I lower the buyer's order. I look him straight in the eye.

I appreciate that, Hezekiah. If more people were honest, I say, selling cars would certainly be a lot more enjoyable. You'd be surprised what sort of junk I pay top dollar for.

He says, "No one can fool you. You're a car salesman."

So many years in church, I say, has made me an easy mark for the false tongue.

"Really? What faith are you?"

I say, It's against policy for me to discuss religion at work.

I could've said, my faith is money—though it didn't used to be.

Even now on Sundays when I'm not slamming customers or stealing the commission from some ignorant green pea, I might visit the Church of Our Blessed Redeemer Who Walked Upon the Waters to check on the Faithful. I arrive late, take a seat in the back, of course, sing as loud as anybody else—without use of a hymnal—the songs I've known since childhood, and then leave as soon as the musical portion ends. I like music. I can pick a tune on the piano with the best of them, but I have no time for sermons anymore and no faith, except for the green kind, since Elaine passed.

One day I left my wife and child and God for her. It was long overdue. I think I was happy. The next day she was hospitalized. No cancer. No heart disease. No high blood pressure whirling out of control. An embolism—whatever that is—in her brain. And then in my heart.

"Love," she said. The green, electric mountains became hills, then smaller hills, and then they flattened against the horizon.

The blip-blip became a sigh.

"What?" I said, leaning close to her ear.

"God is Love," she said. And then she died, even though I held her hand. She was a year shy of sixty.

"You wouldn't be a Holy Roller, would you?" Hezekiah McBride says.

Are you?

With his thumbs, he pulls his pants up higher than his waist. "I'm Pastor of the Greater Miami Holy Rollers' Tabernacle of Faith."

Beaming, I shake his hand.

I lie, I'm a Holy Roller, too!

"Really? I've never seen you in service. Where do you worship?"

I'm not local.

"Kendall, Goulds, Homestead . . . ?"

Yes, Goulds.

(Wherever that is.)

"Pastor Jeroboam, right?"

Yes.

(I guess.)

"Well," he says, "you must come up to Greater Miami next week. We're having a tent meeting, and believe me, brother, you don't want to miss the Rev. Jedediah Witherspoon. He's a dynamic speaker."

Rev. Jedediah Witherspoon, I echo. I've heard of him.

(Who?)

"Well this is something," he says. "To meet a brother at a car dealership."

He made some preachers, He made some salesmen, I say.

"Amen," he says.

I tell you what I'm going to do for you, Pastor McBride. I'm going to simplify this deal. How much do you really think your trade-in is worth?

He knits his brow. "About eight hundred."

A '74 Eldorado with no tires, no grille, and serious rust?

"Five hundred?"

Pastor, it's got over two hundred thousand miles.

"Three hundred?"

A hundred fifty dollars tops, I say.

"That's no deal," he says. "The other guy offered me more."

On paper he did. But when you figured it out . . .

He sighs.

What about this? What if I buy the car from you? What if I give you the hundred fifty in cash? Real money. It's more than these heathens are going to give you when they finish writing it up on paper.

"Cash? Can you do that?" he says.

Yes, I'll buy the car myself. I need something to putter around town in, I say. You can add what I give you to your down payment and get a cheaper monthly rate.

And we don't have to let the dealership know. This is between brothers.

"Amen to that," he says. And Hezekiah McBride, without my asking him to, sits down and once again pulls out his four hundred fifty dollars in tens and twenties; I reach into my wallet and pull out the "biscuit"—the hundred fifty dollars that the dealership gives me for just such occasions.

I give the biscuit to Hezekiah, and he gives it back to me with his down payment. Now he's happy with the deal.

So am I.

Perhaps if Pastor Hezekiah McBride had earned a useless bachelor's degree in mathematics like I did, he'd realize that biscuit or not, I just snatched his trade-in for a hundred dollars less than the Arab was offering him.

$ $ $

"You are on a roll, my friend," says the Arab.

We could've made more money if you hadn't been so transparant.

"Like you're hurtin' for money," Curly says, "after the mint you made on that black girl."

I shouldn't have buried her, I say. It's her first car.

"So?"

She rode in on a bike.

"Don't worry about it," says my manager. "With the money you made, you can afford to take her out to a fancy dinner. Wine her, dine her, take her to bed. I did it a hundred times when I was in sales."

The Arab says, "Best lovers are customers."

Curly says, "Ever notice how when a customer forces a great deal out of you, I mean practically steals the best car on the lot, that this same jerk customer—instead of being satisfied—always returns again and again to complain about everything? But you rip a customer off, bury the sucker like you did that black girl today—and guess what? That customer never bothers you again. If anything, a sucker like that refers other suckers to you."

She's not a sucker, I say.

"No offense," says the Arab, "but you know young black women are the easiest sell. Young black women, then young black men, then young white women, young white men, and like that all the way up to the toughest sell, old white men."

So where do sand-niggers like yourself fit in?

"Hey," exclaims the Arab.

Are kikes on that list?

"Wait a minute," says Curly, rising to his feet—Curly whose paternal grandfather had survived Treblinka.

I turn to my manager, but he is a peckerwood with the power to fire me.

He smiles. "Take it easy," he says, putting a hand on my shoulder.

"You've gone overboard," says Curly. "You wouldn't like it if I called you the N-word."

"I thought we were friends," says the Arab.

Forgive me, I say. You are my friend. You are all my friends. I'm just under a lot of pressure.

"But you made so much money," say the Arab, Curly, and my manager.

Yes, I did, I say.

But maybe money isn't everything.

$ $ $

I pull up to my parents' house, where I live in a room over their garage. A light is on in the living room, and through the verticals I make out my mother, my father, and my ex-wife Mary, who I know is there to ask me in a most displeasing fashion why child support payments haven't been received in two months, so I back up and out of the driveway.

I drive a two-seater tonight, my reward for burying Ida and bamboozling Pastor Hezekiah McBride. The odometer reads 25—a virgin. The smell is Windex and Lysol and something lemony. Then the car smells like smoke, too, when I light a cigarette. I'm trying to quit. I take two, three, four drags and I crumple the cigarette into the ashtray. Then I chew a piece of Juicy Fruit, wad it up, and stick it in the ashtray as a little something for the new owners to find—let them know I was here first. I ride the clutch. I make the tires squeal when I round corners. I pull onto the lonely expressway, pretend it is the Autobahn, crank it up to 120.

As usual, I end up in that bad section of town where Peachie, my oldest and dearest friend, lives. My car is eyed by two lanky, young men with heads shaved except for on the top where there is a profusion of short, tight braids tied together with rubber bands. I get out of the car. I do not bother to lock the doors. It ain't my car. What do I care?

Inside, Peachie lights cherry incense. She goes into the bedroom and comes out in a see-through slip. We fall onto the couch and grope each other until it is obvious nothing more is going to happen.

I light a cigarette.

Peachie rolls off my lap and sits up, scratching her bare ass. "I thought you quit smoking." She makes a prune face and fans the fumes away from her, gets up and mounts her exercise bicycle set up in the middle of the small livingroom—THE AMAZING CENTRO-CYCLE, LOSE TEN POUNDS IN TEN DAYS—actual weight loss may vary from user to user.

She begins to pedal. "Smoking is going to give you cancer."

The spirit is willing, but the flesh is weak.

I take a final puff and mash the cigarette into the bright red ceramic, elephant-fending-off-tiger attack ashtray on her coffee table.

"You're the only one who ever uses that," she observes.

I get up and reach for Peachie again.

She covers her breasts with the see-through slip and shoos me away. "Don't start the engine if you don't want to drive," she quips, pedaling faster. "So talk."

My life is shit.

"Not your life," she says. Pedal. Pedal. "Your job. Just quit your shitty job."

It's not that easy. I love my shitty job. It's great getting paid to play mind games on people.

"It must be, because they certainly don't pay you much. Your ex-wife is hounding you for child support. When was the last time she let you see your son? And look at you—a car salesman who can't afford a car. You're a college graduate, isn't that what they call irony?" Pedal. Pedal. Peachie, my once-skinny Peachie, weighs close to two hundred pounds. But she manages the restaurant now. She's moving out of this dump at the end of the month. In a year, she'll apply for a franchise, and she'll get it. She's that good at what she does.

It beats preaching, I say.

"Who're you kidding? Preachers make plenty of money. And I know from experience that they get laid a lot, too."

It's just a joke, I say.

"The joke is that at thirty-five you still live with your parents."

Thanks for cheering me up, Peachie. I feel so good I could just kill myself. Praise the Lord for friends like you.

"That'll teach you to withhold sex from me. You know how snippy I am when I don't get my quota."

Look, if you're serious about it, I'll come over on the weekend. I'll help you pack and et cetera.

"No dice. The kids are coming down from Anderson. We're going up to Disney World."

You've really gotten your life together, Peachie. I envy you.

"All I had to do was figure out that the Lord wasn't going to help Peachie until Peachie helped Peachie. The solution was on the inside all the time." The big wheel on the bike is turning harder now. Pedal. Pedal. "So who has rendered you impotent this time? A secretary, a fry cook, a bag lady—"

Bag ladies don't buy cars.

"A maid, a postal clerk, a stripper. Strippers buy cars, don't they?"

Yes. I've had a few strippers.

"A ditch digger, a cop, a paralegal . . ."

A student, I say.

"Aha! Seduction of the innocent. Have you slept with her yet?"

No. And I think there may be something more to it this time.

"You?" She gets off the bike, wipes the sweat from her brow with the hem of the slip. Peachie's a big woman now. But her body looks real nice with the extra pounds. Real nice. "Give me a break."

Really. I regret ripping her off.

"Regret? Not you." Now Peachie mimics me: "I feel no guilt. I'm a salesman. I'm hardcore. I've got a hard on for hard cash."

The student reminds me of Elaine.

Peachie opens her lips and sucks in air. Now she says in a soft voice, "In what way?"

It's in the way she cries, she reminds me. I ripped her off, threw it in her face, and yet she doesn't hate me.

"Turning the other cheek," Peachie says. "So much like Christ."

Not funny, Sister McGowan.

"I couldn't resist. Why did you rip her off?"

Blinded by greed, I guess.

"It's not greed if they don't pay you shit," she says. "Blinded by stupidity most likely." Peachie kisses me on the forehead. "Go after her."

Yeah. I'm thinking the same thing.

"And make amends."

I no longer subscribe to the concept of guilt. It is not by your works ye are saved, Peachie. But I'm thinking the same thing.

"And get out of the car business. It's taking your soul."

I no longer subscribe to the concept of a soul or a God, Peachie, but I'm thinking the same thing.

Peachie slaps my mouth playfully. "Liar, liar, liar. You're just as much a Christian as you've ever been."

What proof do you have that this is so?

She says, "Your life, in fact, is shit, but you're still able to love."

· I think about this for a few moments, then I say, Good answer, Peachie. Good answer.

"God is Love," Peachie says.

$ $ $

So here I am the next morning, fighting with Lou the service writer. First he tells me the Lord of Travel is going to have to wait its turn in line. The mechanics won't get to it until late tomorrow. They won't finish it until late the day after that. It's going to cost at least $400.

Four bills? I know you can fix it for less than four bills, I say. The car is for my "mother," Lou. I'm sure you can do it for less than four bills, and don't give me that crap about waiting in line. We work together, Lou.

Lou says, "What can I do? I don't own the business. I don't make the rules."

I know, I know, I say. But remember, Lou, I covered for you on that tires and batteries thing, and all I asked for was a measly twenty when I could've asked for fifty or a hundred. Remember, Lou, one hand washes the other.

Lou remembers the tires and batteries thing. "I'll see what I can do," he says, "for your mother."

At 1 p.m., Lou calls me.

I run to the service area and pay my "mother's" tab, $50 in cash, which I hand Lou and which he puts in his wallet.

The Lord of Travel does not emit smoke nor spray water anymore, but I notice it pulls too much to the left. When it runs, I can hear its belts grinding. It stalls, once in a while, in idle. I worry about the brakes, which are slow to respond. I take it back to Lou, who is not happy to see me but smiles anyway.

My mother says the car needs a tune-up, new belts, a new battery, new brake shoes, I tell him. She travels out of town a lot and wants to feel secure on the road. By the way, she was wondering if you could check the alignment and, if it's not too much trouble, throw a couple tires in the trunk. The ones in back are just about worn out.

"Your mother is a thief," Lou says.

And she needs it by five . . . today.

"My God."

It's just a little favor, Lou.

He whispers, "OK. But after this, no more. We're even."

Sure, Lou.

"No. To hell with that. Now you owe me."

I'll take care of you, I say. I know a few people who could use a discounted set of tires, no questions asked.

$ $ $

They finish the Lord of Travel just after 4 p.m. I take it for a test drive, and I am impressed. Lou had them put over a thousand dollars worth of parts and labor into the car in less than seven hours. And all for $50 and a smile! The car wasn't so bad after all. It just needed to have a few specific parts repaired.

I take it across the street to the Amoco station where I fill it with gas using the dealership's credit card. Then I slide Miguel $5, and he washes and waxes it until I can see my reflection—I am framed in a shave, a haircut, a new tie. I'm not so bad either.

Curly pats me on the back. "Lookin' good. I hope the sex is worth all this."

I'm not after sex this time.

"Is she rich?" says the Arab.

It's not like that, I say. This is my last day.

"Yeah?" says the Arab. "Where you headed this time? Buick? Izuzu? Honda?" He reads something in my expression that is not there. "Aha, so big bonus Mike over at Honda got your attention again."

Curly says, "It's not a bad idea. They pay thirty percent after the tenth car."

"Thirty percent?" says the Arab. "Really?" He licks his lips, looks at me.

I have no idea, I say. I'm not going to Honda. I'm not going anywhere. One good deed for this woman, and then I'm gone. I'm getting out of the business.

"Out of the business? No way," says the Arab. "Once a car salesman, always a car salesman. It's like religion."

"What will you do for money?" says Curly.

Anything but this, I say. I'll flip hamburgers. I'll paint houses. I need a real job. I'll sell Amway.

"No way," says the Arab. "You'll never quit."

"And why would you want to quit?" Curly says. I am sandwiched between them. A determined hand on each of my shoulders keeps me from moving. "Why quit after you made so much money? Is it this girl?"

Of course. It's always a girl.

$ $ $

When Ida arrives, she does so in a car driven by a large, hairy man whose face is a mask of hatefulness. As the car rolls by, she points to me and the angry man gives me a look that leaves no doubt he wants to hurt me, so I toss Miguel the keys and run inside the showroom.

Take care of her, I say. Tell her I'm in a meeting and can't be disturbed.

Inside I watch, hidden behind the Arab, who always carries a can of mace, and big Curly, who was on his college wrestling team before he flunked out.

Ida and the man park next to the Lord of Travel. They get out and slam their doors. The man runs his hands over the car. He seems pleased with what he discovers, and his expression softens somewhat. He looks at Ida, who shrugs her shoulders. She grabs the keys from Miguel, and she and the large man hop into the Lord of Travel and spin off for a test drive. Nearly an hour later, they return. The large man gets into his car and drives away without a word to Ida.

Ida stands beside the Lord of Travel, perplexed. I walk out to meet her.

"He likes the car," she says. "He had one like it when he was younger."

(Probably the same one.)

I told you it was a nice car, I say. You see, I am a nice guy. I had them fix it up for you and everything. And I paid for it out of my own pocket.

"I bet you did," she says.

I really did.

"But you overcharged me for it in the first place."

I tried to get you the best deal I could.

"I bet you did."

I really did.

"Doesn't matter. If he says it's a nice car, it's a nice car."

He's your . . . mechanic?

"My boyfriend."

Lucky guy, I say.

"He came to get my money back. And if necessary," she says, her eyes narrowing to slits, "to beat the hell out of you."

Lucky me, I think. But I know she would never let him hurt me, this hairy man she claims is her boyfriend. She brought him because she knows what I am capable of, and she wanted a fair fight this time. Smart.

Ida is beautiful. I want to hear her say that I'm not like the rest of them. I want another hug. I want to love her.

So I say, well you got yourself a nice car though, didn't you?

I nod my head. She nods hers.

All your friends will be impressed, won't they?

I nod my head. She nods hers.

And, I add, you made a new friend, didn't you?

I nod my head and extend my hand, but she only looks at me and laughs.

She says, "It never ends with you people, does it?"

No, I say. I'm not like that anymore. I quit. I really did.

"Lucky you," she says, and then she gets into the refurbished Lord of Travel and drives away, leaving me standing there with my hand extended.

I think, God is Love, God is Love, God is Love.

I am so choked up that the Arab almost beats me to the next customer who pulls up on the lot. But I can tell by the cut of the man's double-breasted jacket and his confident, purposeful stride that he's on mission. That he's a preacher. The poor Arab doesn't have a chance.

I move so fast I must have wings.